Nell hel

Zack's fing   rom
the soft cur   egan
to touch his   she
was doing,

'You can't hold your breath for ever,' he told
her at last. 'What do you suppose is going to
happen when you breathe out, Nell?'

Dear Reader

For many of us, this is the best period of the year—the season of goodwill and celebration—though it can make big demands on your time and pocket, too! Or, maybe you prefer to spend these mid-winter months more quietly? Whatever you've got planned, Mills & Boon's romances are always there for you as special friends at the turn of the year: easy, entertaining and comforting reads that are great value for money. Stay warm, won't you!

The Editor

Joanna Mansell hasn't always wanted to write. It was an idea that popped into her head when she was 'thirty-something', and then wouldn't go away again. It's turned out to be rather addictive, though, and now she has started, she says, she can't stop! When she's not working, she loves reading, gardening, watching films, daydreaming, and sneaking away from the typewriter on hot, sunny days to go for walks along the sea front.

SECRETS OF
THE NIGHT

BY

JOANNA MANSELL

MILLS & BOON LIMITED
ETON HOUSE   18-24 PARADISE ROAD
RICHMOND   SURREY   TW9 1SR

All the characters in this book have no existence outside the imagination of the Author, and have no relation whatsoever to anyone bearing the same name or names. They are not even distantly inspired by any individual known or unknown to the Author, and all the incidents are pure invention.

All Rights Reserved. The text of this publication or any part thereof may not be reproduced or transmitted in any form or by any means, electronic or mechanical, including photocopying, recording, storage in an information retrieval system, or otherwise, without the written permission of the publisher.

This book is sold subject to the condition that it shall not, by way of trade or otherwise, be lent, resold, hired out or otherwise circulated without the prior consent of the publisher in any form of binding or cover other than that in which it is published and without a similar condition including this condition being imposed on the subsequent purchaser.

*First published in Great Britain 1992
by Mills & Boon Limited*

© Joanna Mansell 1992

*Australian copyright 1992
Philippine copyright 1993
This edition 1993*

ISBN 0 263 77864 9

*Set in Times Roman 10 on 12 pt.
01-9301-50194 C*

Made and printed in Great Britain

CHAPTER ONE

As SHE drove through the golden, sunlit hills of Tuscany, Nell was so tired that she almost didn't notice the man sitting at the side of the road, with blood steadily dripping from his arm and his forehead.

He slowly raised his head as she drove past, and she had gone another couple of hundred yards before she realised what she had just seen. Her foot slammed down on the brakes, the car slewed to a halt on the narrow, dusty road, then she hurriedly threw it into reverse.

As the car rather erratically raced backwards, Nell could feel her pulses thumping. What on earth had happened to him? An accident? An assault of some kind?

She brought the car to a halt alongside him, and then took a closer look. Her heart sank when she saw his deeply tanned skin and his dark, almost black hair. A local man, she decided with a worried frown. And her Italian was almost non-existent.

She hastily ran through the dozen or so 'useful phrases' that she had memorised on the plane, trying to find something appropriate. Unfortunately, none of the useful sentences mentioned a man sitting, bleeding, beside the road! Nell gave a rather shaky sigh and got out of the car.

As she walked over to the man, he raised his head and looked at her. His eyes were a vivid blue, and slightly unfocused.

'Er—*come sta*?' she said rather nervously.

'How am I?' he muttered, in a caustic tone. 'Unless you're half blind or an imbecile, I'd have thought that was fairly obvious!'

Not Italian, she realised at once. Apart from anything else, an Italian man wouldn't have been so rude.

'You're English?' she asked.

'Is that important? Do you check on everyone's nationality before you offer to help them?' he enquired sarcastically.

Nell was seriously beginning to wonder if she wanted to help this man at all! She could hardly leave him sitting by the side of the road, though. Not many people used this route; it could be hours before someone else came along and offered assistance.

She forced herself to ignore his rudeness and said in a more practical tone of voice, 'Can you stand up? If not, I'll try and help you to your feet.'

He looked back at her sceptically. 'You don't look strong enough to help a mouse to its feet, let alone a fully grown man.'

This man definitely had an attitude problem, she decided, any sympathy she had felt towards him because of his injuries rapidly beginning to drain away. 'Look, if you don't want any help, just come right out and say so,' she said with a touch of exasperation. 'Or if it's just *my* help that you don't want, that's OK with me. I'll just leave you here. You can sit and wait for someone else to come along. Only you might have a very long wait,' she warned him. 'This road only leads to a couple of isolated farmhouses, and it might be hours before another car passes by.'

A dark look crossed the man's face. 'All right, I get the message,' he growled.

'I just don't think you're being very helpful,' she pointed out.

'The fact that my head hurts like hell might have something to do with it. I can't even think straight, let alone make an effort to be polite.'

Nell immediately regretted her own prickly response. It was just that this man had chosen a bad time to expect help from her. Her life was in such a mess at the moment that she wasn't even sure she could help herself, let alone someone else.

'Look, let's start over again,' she said in a more friendly voice. 'Try and stand up. If you can make it, then I'll help you get into the car.'

The man slowly hauled himself to his feet. When he had finally managed it, Nell took an involuntary step backwards. She hadn't expected him to be quite so tall. She had intended to offer him her shoulder to lean on, but at the last moment something stopped her. Perhaps it was the way this man loomed over her, physically intimidating despite his injuries. She suddenly knew she wanted to keep a safe distance away from him.

He lurched towards the car, slumped into the front seat, then gave an audible sigh of relief and closed his eyes.

'Just take me with you, wherever you're going, bandage me up and then find me somewhere to sleep for a few hours,' he said in a weary voice.

Warning bells instantly rang inside Nell's head. As far as she was concerned, that definitely wasn't a good idea. 'I can't take you with me,' she told him bluntly.

His eyes flickered open again. 'Why not?' Then his vivid blue gaze narrowed. 'Jealous husband at home? That won't be a problem—I'm not in any fit state to seduce you.'

'I haven't got a husband.' She knew at once that it had been a mistake to tell him that. His blue eyes immediately focused on her more sharply as he considered her admission.

'You're here in Italy on your own?' he said at last.

He made it sound as if she hadn't been able to find one single person, male or female, who had wanted to come with her. Nell's self-esteem, already at rock bottom, somehow managed to sink even lower.

'There's nothing wrong with being on my own, is there?' she said rather defiantly.

'No,' he agreed. 'But for a girl who looks like you, it's—unusual.'

For some reason it disturbed her that, despite his injuries, he had noticed how she looked.

'I don't care if it's unusual or not,' she said, her voice much sharper than she had intended. 'I'm on my own because that's the way I *want* to be at the moment. It's also the reason why I can't take you with me.'

He looked at her thoughtfully. 'You're frightened of me?'

'Of course not!' she denied at once, conveniently forgetting her odd, nervous reaction when he had stood up and loomed over her. 'But I don't pick up perfect strangers and take them home with me. For a woman on her own, that would be an extremely stupid thing to do.'

The stranger looked at her thoughtfully. 'You don't feel safe with me?' he said at last.

'I don't even know you,' Nell pointed out. 'I don't have the slightest idea who you are, or why you were sitting by the side of the road, bleeding all over the place.'

'Came off my motorbike,' he told her economically, as if talking required rather more energy than he had left. 'Swerved to avoid a dog, and hit a rock instead.'

'I don't see a dog *or* a motorbike,' she said, looking around suspiciously.

He pointed towards a narrow track that joined the road a few yards further on.

'It happened a couple of hundred yards up there. I managed to walk down to the road—I thought I'd be able to find someone who would help.'

'And you found me.' She couldn't keep a note of regret out of her voice. She felt sorry for him, but a problem like this really was the very last thing she needed right now.

'I apologise if it's inconvenient.' His voice was becoming a little slurred, and she looked at him with some alarm.

'You're not going to pass out, are you?'

'Probably not, but I can't guarantee it.'

'But you haven't even told me your name yet!'

'Can't remember it.'

Nell stared at him. 'You don't know who you are?'

'It's only temporary. Everything will come back once I've had some rest.'

'How can you be sure of that?' she asked with fresh nervousness. She wasn't at all sure she could cope with an injured man who didn't even know who he was!

He held up his hands. 'I can see five fingers,' he told her. 'I know what day of the week it is, and I even know roughly where I am—somewhere between Florence and Siena. I remember swerving to avoid that damned dog, and I *definitely* remember hitting the ground after coming off the bike. It's just a few odd details that I can't recall.'

'Like your name!'

'Is it important?'

'It seems pretty important to me.' Her big brown eyes looked even more worried as she looked at him again. 'You keep going very pale. I think you need to see a doctor.'

'No, I don't,' he said at once. 'I just need to sleep for a few hours. Look, if you're too nervous to let me inside your house, leave me in the car. I can easily stretch out on the back seat.'

'Why don't you want to see a doctor?' she asked with a small frown.

'I don't like them.'

'How do you know that, if you can't remember anything?'

'I told you, I can remember some things. And I certainly remember that I don't like doctors.' His voice began to slur a little again. 'Anyway, do you know where to find one?' he muttered, his eyes closing.

She didn't. 'There must be someone we can ask,' she argued. When he didn't reply, she looked at him more closely and was alarmed to find that he was either asleep or unconscious.

She ran her fingers rather distractedly through her long dark hair. What on earth was she meant to do now?

Her choices seemed very limited. She could take him with her, to the farmhouse that she was heading for, or she could try and find someone else who could look after this semi-conscious man.

She looked around rather anxiously. The sun was already sliding behind the low hills, which meant it would soon be night. She would have to reach a decision fairly soon.

In the end, she started up the car again and began to drive. She was renting the farmhouse for a couple of weeks, and the booking agent had told her the owner would be waiting for her, to give her the keys, tell her where everything was, and give her any more information she might need. If she took this man with her, the owner of the farmhouse would be able to give her the help she needed. He would know the phone number of the nearest doctor, in case the bruises and bloodstains covered more serious injuries, and he would probably know someone who would give this stranger a bed for a night or two.

Feeling better now that she had reached a definite decision, Nell began to drive faster. According to the map she had been following, it was only another couple of kilometres before she reached the farmhouse. Then she could hand this man and all his problems over to someone else.

As she drove off, she shook her head in disbelief that something like this could have happened. At the moment, she seemed to be attracting trouble and problems like a magnet! She had fled to this quiet corner of Tuscany because she had desperately needed a few days of peace and solitude, to try and get her shattered life back into some kind of order. She had just been through a very bad couple of weeks—most of which had been her fault, she reminded herself grimly—and she had needed this time to herself to try and get herself together again. Here she was, though, facing another crisis, although admittedly a very minor one compared to what she had been through recently. She didn't want *any* kind of complications in her life at the moment, though. All she craved was tranquillity and seclusion.

She had also firmly resolved to avoid any involvement with men while she was in Italy. After her recent disastrous experience, it was going to be a very long time before she was ready for another relationship. Even if the most incredibly tall, dark and handsome man wandered by, she was determined to look the other way. At least, that had been her intention. She hadn't counted on finding that tall, handsome man slumped by the side of the road!

Nell glanced with fresh unease at her passenger. *Was* he handsome? It was hard to tell, but she had the unnerving feeling that the bruises and bloodstains hid the features of one of the most gorgeous-looking men she had ever seen. And he was certainly overwhelmingly male from the top of his dark head to his toes.

She hastily looked back at the road again. It doesn't matter what he looks like, she told herself firmly. You're just going to give him whatever help he needs, then concentrate on your own problems, on getting your own life back into some kind of order.

The car purred onwards, through the beautiful but deserted Tuscan countryside. Nell had asked the travel agent to find her somewhere peaceful and isolated, but she was beginning to wish he hadn't been quite so successful! Of course, when she had arranged to rent the farmhouse, she hadn't expected to have an injured stranger with her. Nell gave a deep sigh. Picking up a strange man and taking him home with her definitely wasn't a sensible thing to do. What would her parents say if they ever found out?

Then she gave another, more resigned sigh. They would probably say nothing at all. After everything that had happened over the last couple of weeks, she guessed they had been left practically speechless!

She decided she wouldn't even tell them about this little episode; she had caused them enough worry and heartache recently. Anyway, as soon as she reached the farmhouse the problem would be out of her hands. The owner of the farmhouse would take responsibility for this stranger, and deal with all his problems.

Almost as if he knew she was thinking about him, the man beside her stirred. Nell shot a brief look at him. Even with his features relaxed, there was something about this man that looked intimidating, she decided nervously. And it didn't really have anything to do with the powerful set of his body. It was more in the stern lines of his face, the stubborn set of his jaw, the dark brows that framed those vivid blue eyes.

Slightly alarmed that she had noticed so much about him, she swivelled her gaze back to the road again. She wasn't interested in what he looked like, she told herself stubbornly. She just wanted to patch him up, then get him out of her life!

The car bumped on along the uneven road, and the sun sank further behind the hills, leaving a dark golden glow in the sky. Rows of tall, thin cypresses were etched against the horizon, and the distant walls and jumbled skyline of a small hill town began to fade into the shadows. Small motes of dust hung in the still evening air, and swallows swooped overhead, catching their last crop of midges before flying off to find a safe perch for the night.

The road curved upwards, and Nell knew she was almost there. One more bend and she would have reached the farmhouse. She manoeuvred the car round the last corner, then brought it to a halt with a relieved sigh. The farmhouse was directly in front of her, the stone walls and terracotta roof catching the golden light still radiating from the sinking sun, so that they glowed warmly and welcomingly. Geraniums and petunias tumbled in bright, gaudy colours out of the tubs that flanked the front entrance, and a climbing rose smothered in rich cream blossoms reached almost to the roof.

Nell cut the engine and jumped out. It was perfect, she decided happily as her gaze drifted over the farmhouse and the soft sweep of the hills that surrounded it. All she had to do now was to find the owner and introduce herself.

She had expected him to come out and meet her. There was no sign of anyone, though, so she decided he must still be inside the farmhouse. Perhaps he hadn't heard the car.

As she walked towards the front door, though, she noticed the sheet of paper taped just above the knocker. Apprehension fluttered through her nerve-ends, deepening into a quick shiver as she read the note. The writing was bold and distinctive.

Sorry, but I had to leave early. The keys are behind the flowerpot to the right of the door. Enjoy your stay here.

The note ended in an indecipherable signature, but Nell was no longer looking at it.

'The owner isn't here,' she muttered to herself edgily. 'So—what are you going to do now?'

The trouble was, her choices seemed very limited. She could hardly take the man back to where she had found him, and leave him by the side of the road. And he had said he only wanted somewhere to rest for a few hours, until he had got over the worst effects of his accident. Perhaps she could let him stay here for just one night. He could sleep in the car; she wouldn't even have to let him inside the house.

Reluctantly Nell walked back to the car. As she opened the door, the man stirred, then opened his eyes.

'Have we arrived?'

'Yes,' she said, then added quickly, 'I think you'd better stay where you are. It's better not to move when you're injured. I'll find a couple of blankets, so you can make yourself comfortable.'

His dark eyebrows slowly rose. 'You don't want me inside the house?'

'You did say you wouldn't mind sleeping in the car,' Nell reminded him.

'I've changed my mind about that. I want to go inside, find a soft, warm bed, and collapse into it.'

'But I don't *want* you inside,' she said with a fresh burst of nervousness.

'You've no reason to be scared of me,' he told her, looking directly at her.

'I'm n-not scared of you,' she said, her slight stammer immediately giving away the fact that she was lying. 'But you know I'm here by myself. I don't think it's a very good idea to let you inside the house. For all I know, you could be a criminal, or the sort of man who likes preying on women on their own.'

His mouth set into a warning line. 'I'm neither of those things,' he growled.

'How do you know, if you can't remember anything?' Nell challenged him.

'I haven't forgotten everything,' he replied, his blue eyes still looking straight at her. 'I know very well the kind of man I am.'

She looked away from him because, for some reason, she found it very difficult to stare into that bright blue gaze for too long. 'You could be wrong about yourself,' she insisted stubbornly. 'And haven't you made a rather miraculous recovery in these last couple of minutes?' she added suspiciously. 'A little while ago you were almost out cold. Now you're talking your head off!'

'I wasn't out cold, I was simply resting. But I can't guarantee that I won't pass out, if you leave me out here on my own. I could develop concussion and lie unconscious for hours, and no one would even know about it.'

'That's blackmail,' she told him with some annoyance.

An unexpected gleam lit his eyes. 'I simply think of it as a way of making sure I get a comfortable bed for the night.'

'Men!' she exclaimed with sudden fierceness. 'You're all the same! Why do you have to play games to get what you want? Why can't you be straightforward and honest?'

'Like women?' he suggested softly. 'But women can play the most complicated—and cruellest—games of all.'

For a moment she stared at him. Had some woman played a game with *him*? It was hard to believe that. She was quite sure it would take a very clever woman indeed to get the better of this man.

'I'm not complicated or cruel,' she said at last in a low voice.

'Then you'll give me a bed for the night?' he said in a more relaxed tone.

Nell felt as if she had been neatly boxed into a corner, and she wasn't sure how it had happened.

'I don't really have any choice, do I?' she muttered. And it was true. How could she leave an injured man lying cramped up in a small car all night? 'You'd better wait here for a couple of minutes,' she added reluctantly. 'I'll go and open up the house.'

She collected her luggage from the boot, searched behind the flowerpot for the key to the farmhouse and, when she had found it, slid it into the lock, which clicked open easily. The heavy door swung open, and she went inside.

Her gaze drifted with pleasure over the light colour-washed walls, and tiled floors, the dark, exposed beams

in the ceiling overhead, and the plain, functional furniture. This was the kind of house where you could feel
relaxed and at home as soon as you walked in the door.
At least, she *would* have felt relaxed if that dark-haired
stranger hadn't been waiting out in the car.

Was she mad, letting him into the house? Nell had
the uneasy feeling that it wasn't the wisest decision she
had ever made. One more stupid act to add to all the
very foolish things she had done recently.

She tried to comfort herself with the thought that it
would only be for one night. He would sleep for a few
hours, then he would go. She would finally be on her
own, and she could set about the task of trying to re-
store herself, physically and mentally, to some vestige of
the way she had used to be.

Now that the decision had been made, she walked
briskly back out to the man in her car. She found he
had closed his eyes again, and seemed to be asleep.

Rather gingerly she reached out and gently touched
him with just one finger. When he didn't respond, she
sighed again and gave him a brief shake, letting go of
him again as soon as he stirred.

His eyes opened, his bright blue gaze fixed on her,
and she knew at once that he hadn't been asleep, as she
had supposed. 'You didn't want to touch me, did you?'
he said, looking up at her thoughtfully.

'What on earth are you talking about?' she queried
in a wary voice.

'You behaved as if just touching me would burn your
fingers.' His eyes narrowed and he looked at her ques-
tioningly. 'What's the matter? Don't you like men?'

'The way I feel about men—about anything—is absolutely none of your business,' she retorted, far more sharply than was necessary.

'I thought that might be the reason you're here by yourself,' he suggested softly. 'You're hiding away from the male population. Or from one particular man?'

'I'm not hiding away from anything or anyone,' Nell lied, rather unnerved by the accuracy of his guess.

'Oh, yes, you are,' he said in that same quiet voice. 'And I'd like to know why.'

'I'm sure you'd like to know a lot of things, but I'm not going to answer any of your questions,' she retorted with some determination. 'I'm offering you a bed for the night, not the story of my life. You can either take up that offer or you can spend the night here, in the car.'

A sudden gleam lit his eyes. 'I'm not sure if I can walk as far as the house without some help.'

'If you can't manage on your own, I'm sure I can find you a walking stick,' Nell said at once.

'You're not offering a shoulder to lean on?'

'I've already told you I'm not offering anything at all, except somewhere to rest for the night. *One* night,' she added pointedly.

'What a prickly girl you're turning out to be. Like a small porcupine, bristling in every direction.'

'And you want some tender loving care? Sorry, but it's not on offer,' Nell said abruptly. 'I'm clean out of it at the moment. You've caught me at the wrong time and in the wrong mood.'

'That's fairly obvious.' His blue gaze rested on her with new interest. 'Why aren't you in the mood for it?'

'That's something else that's none of your business.' Nell knew she was being rude, but the sudden personal questions were beginning to unsettle her. She could feel herself glaring at him, and tried to stop herself. She had the feeling it wouldn't be wise to antagonise this man.

She reminded herself that he *was* injured, and deserved sympathy, not hostility. 'Are you coming into the house?' she asked, making an effort to keep her voice more polite.

He levered himself out of the car, and she was relieved to find that he seemed to be able to walk unaided, although he was still slightly unsteady on his feet. Inside the farmhouse, stone steps led up to the first floor and, Nell guessed, to the bedrooms. She turned in the opposite direction, though. She didn't want him installed in one of the bedrooms. There must be a couch he could sleep on. He would be perfectly comfortable there—and *she* would feel a lot safer!

She went through a doorway on the far side of the entrance hall, then breathed a small sigh of relief. The small sitting-room had a heavy wooden dresser against one wall, a table and chairs in the same dark wood, and a large couch with a brightly coloured cover thrown over it. This was a very suitable room for him to spend the night.

Nell switched on the lamp, which made the room seem even more cosy. Then she turned to the man, who had followed her more slowly.

'You can sleep here tonight,' she told him. 'Is there anything you need?'

'Several things,' he told her, making his way over to the couch and collapsing on to it with some relief. 'Firstly, a bandage or plaster, so I don't drip blood all over this couch. And I haven't had anything to eat for a long time. I don't suppose you've got anything to drink?' he added.

'There's probably tea and coffee in the kitchen.'

'That wasn't quite what I had in mind,' he said drily.

Nell was about to say she would go and look, to see if she could find him something to drink, but then changed her mind. She decided she would prefer it if this man stayed completely sober.

Instead, she began to back towards the door.

'I'll go and try to find some bandages,' she told him. 'There must be a basic first-aid kit somewhere.'

'I'll look for it, if you like?' he offered with unexpected helpfulness.

'No, thank you,' Nell said at once. She didn't want him wandering around the farmhouse. She wanted him to stay exactly where he was, until he left here first thing tomorrow morning. She would feel a little better about this situation if she knew he was confined to one room.

She went upstairs, breathing a little easier once she was well away from him. When she was near to him, there seemed to be something about him that made her feel—well, rather uncomfortable. Of course, that was only to be expected, she told herself hurriedly. In the circumstances, it would be strange if she *didn't* feel like that. All the same, she wished he were much less tall, less powerfully built. And there was something about his eyes, a dark glint that seemed able to make something inside her tremble . . .

Nell quickly suppressed a small shiver and told herself to stop being so ridiculous. Find the bandages, patch him up, let him get a few hours' sleep, then tell him he had to leave. That was all she had to do. If she stuck to that plan, there wouldn't be any problems.

It didn't take her long to find a roll of bandage and a packet of sticking plasters. She gathered them together, then reluctantly went back downstairs.

She went to the room where she had left him—then stopped dead. He wasn't there! But he couldn't have gone. Until he had got some rest, he wouldn't be able to walk much further than the front door. Where was he, though?

With all her nerve-ends twitching, she turned round and marched out of the room, determined to find him.

It didn't take long. The back entrance to the house was open, and she could see his tall, dark figure standing just outside, on the small terrace.

Nell stood in the doorway and frowned at him. 'What are you doing out here?' she demanded.

'Getting some fresh air,' he said easily. 'And enjoying the darkness.'

Oh, yes, she thought to herself, this was a man who would like the night. The soft, sensual warmth, the velvet shadows, the subtle scents and gentle whispers—those bright blue eyes looked as if they knew all the secrets of the night.

'I think you should come back inside,' she said in a crisp voice. *She* certainly wasn't going to be seduced by the dark enchantment of the evening.

He turned and looked at her. 'Does the night make you nervous?' he asked softly.

'Of course not,' Nell said at once, although just a little too vehemently. 'I'm not a child, I'm not scared of the dark.'

'But you are on edge all the time,' he said thoughtfully. 'You keep saying you're not frightened of me, and you're not nervous of the dark, so what's making you so jumpy?'

'I'm not jumpy,' she denied stubbornly. 'Nothing scares me.'

That was a downright lie, of course. Over the past couple of weeks the gutter Press had certainly scared her, with their utter determination to probe into every private corner of her life; the way they had hounded her relentlessly, hell-bent on getting a story. Even more than that, though, just lately she had frightened herself. Been frightened by the way that she had pursued her own ambitions so resolutely that she hadn't even realised what was going on around her. Been frightened by the way she had gone single-mindedly in pursuit of fame and success . . .

'I must have been crazy,' she whispered.

'What did you do that was crazy?' asked the man, in a low and unexpectedly persuasive voice.

Nell jumped at the sound of his voice. For those few moments she had blotted out everything—including him.

And she hadn't realised he had heard her mumble that short sentence.

She got her raw, bruised nerves back under control and fixed a deliberately detached gaze on him.

'I don't want to talk about it, and especially not to you. I want you to come inside so I can bandage those cuts. Then you can go to bed.'

She knew she was being rude and unfriendly, but she couldn't seem to help it. She was no longer the kind, generous, trusting girl she had been a few weeks ago. Some of it was her fault, she freely admitted that, but not all of it. Her good qualities had been taken advantage of in a calculating, callous way, and she wasn't sure she was ever going to be quite the same person again.

She turned round, ready to go back into the farmhouse herself. Then she came to an abrupt halt again. Iron-hard fingers had slid round her arm, preventing her from going any further.

'I think, before you go anywhere, you should apologise.' The man's voice had a new, steely note in it. Something about it made Nell swallow hard, but she was determined not to cringe or back away.

'Apologise?' she echoed defiantly. 'Whatever for?'

'For your attitude, which leaves a great deal to be desired.'

'I don't think I've done anything for which I need to apologise. I stopped to help you, I've brought you to this farmhouse, and I'm letting you stay here tonight, even though it *is* against my better judgement!'

His forefinger moved against her skin in a small movement that might almost have been a caress. Nell fought hard to suppress a brief shiver, but didn't quite manage it.

'So that's it,' he murmured. 'You *are* scared of me. You don't like the thought of me staying here overnight, do you? That's why you're jumpy and hostile.'

She tried to deny it, but couldn't. The physical closeness of this man unnerved her in a way that was entirely new to her.

'Let go of me,' she finally managed to get out in a strangled voice.

Immediately he released her arm. Nell retreated a couple of steps, then glared at him.

'Don't touch me again,' she said angrily.

'I promise I won't lay another finger on you,' he told her levelly. 'You're perfectly safe with me.'

And the funny thing was that she believed him. That didn't stop her from reacting sharply, though.

'I suppose I can't throw you out, it's getting late and it's dark outside. But you can bandage your own cuts,' she told him fiercely, 'get your own supper, then put yourself to bed.'

'That's fine by me,' he said in a completely unruffled tone. 'In fact, I'll feel a lot safer cutting my own bandages—your hands are shaking too much to hold a pair of scissors.'

Nell thrust her trembling hands behind her back, and her brown eyes glowed even brighter.

'By the time I get up in the morning, I want to find you've gone. If you're still here, I'll—I'll——'

'Call the police?' he suggested helpfully. 'I speak fluent Italian, if you need any help with the language.'

Nell gritted her teeth together. Now he was *laughing* at her. She tossed back her long dark hair and walked over to the door. Then she stopped and turned to look at him, holding her head up high, as if trying to convince him that she was completely in charge of the situation, even though they both knew perfectly well that she wasn't.

'Enjoy your joke, but remember, you're leaving first thing in the morning,' she warned him. Then she turned her back on him and walked off, pretending all the time that she couldn't feel that amused blue gaze watching her until she was out of sight.

CHAPTER TWO

NELL went straight upstairs, took a quick look at the bedrooms, and decided which one she wanted to use for the next couple of weeks. It had a large double bed with a wrought-iron headboard, but that was just about the only thing in the room that was in the least fancy. The rest of the furniture, including the cavernous wardrobe, the solid chest of drawers, the small table and the chair by the window, was plain and homely. The room felt comfortable, though, the kind of place where you could relax, and that was very important to her at the moment.

She hauled her case inside, and as she closed the door behind her she was relieved to find that there was a very solid bolt on it. She would feel a lot better with that heavy bolt between her and the man sleeping downstairs.

With a small sigh, she moved over to the window. She stood there for a couple of minutes, feeling the tension in the back of her neck and her shoulders. Finally she raised her arms and lifted the heavy weight of her hair from the nape of her neck. Cool air drifted over her hot skin and she began to relax slightly. Tomorrow would be a better day, she promised herself. The man downstairs would be gone, and she could let the peace and solitude of this place sweep over her, healing some of the damage that had been done lately to her nervous system.

She stepped back, drew the curtains, and began to get ready for bed, suddenly very tired. After a quick shower, she crawled between the clean cotton sheets and closed her heavy, aching eyes. She fell asleep almost immediately, and slept surprisingly well, considering everything that had happened. When she finally woke up the next morning, she stretched luxuriously, and smiled happily to herself as she saw the sunshine filtering through the thin curtains. She was in Italy, the weather was glorious, this was——

She had been about to tell herself that this was the kind of place where she could forget about all her problems and concentrate on getting her life back into order again. But it wasn't! Downstairs, asleep on the couch, was a man who shouldn't be there.

If he was well enough to walk, then he would have to leave, she told herself with determination. She jumped out of bed and pulled on some clean clothes, not even bothering to wash first. She dragged a brush through the worst of the tangles in her hair, then left the bedroom and hurried downstairs.

She went straight to the room with the couch, where the man had spent the night. Without even knocking, she pushed open the door.

The couch had been slept on—the cover was rumpled—but apart from that, there was no sign of him.

Nell looked around suspiciously. Where had he gone? Then she began to relax just a little. He must have phoned for a taxi and already left. Not surprising, really, considering the fact that she hadn't exactly made him welcome. A pang of guilt shot through her as she remembered just how unfriendly and even downright rude she had been. Then she quickly stifled it. Her reaction was perfectly reasonable, under the circumstances, she argued with herself. Sharing this isolated farmhouse with a complete stranger was enough to set anyone's nerves on edge, and make them behave badly.

'You smell nice this morning,' murmured a male voice in her ear. 'Warm and sleepy, as if you've just got out of bed.'

Nell jumped so violently that her feet almost left the ground.

'Don't you *ever* creep up on me again!' she exclaimed furiously, as soon as she had recovered enough to say anything at all.

His dark eyebrows rose gently. 'I never creep anywhere. Perhaps you're hard of hearing?' he suggested helpfully. 'That's why you didn't hear me.'

'There's absolutely nothing wrong with my hearing,' Nell denied, all her nerves still twitching painfully. 'And you *did* creep,' she added in an accusing tone.

He shrugged casually. 'If I made you jump, then I'm sorry.'

'I don't think you're sorry at all—about anything!'

His blue eyes began to look a little less amused. 'Apart from creeping up on you, what else am I supposed to have done?'

'It's what you haven't done,' Nell told him, her brown eyes flashing. 'You haven't left. You're still here!'

'Of course I am. What did you expect me to do? Rush off at the crack of dawn?'

'Yes,' she said heatedly. She knew she was being completely unreasonable, but she couldn't seem to help it. Quite suddenly, she just wanted him *out* of here.

He walked further into the room and sat on the edge of the couch, as if he still found it tiring to stand for any length of time. His skin was a much healthier colour this morning, though, and his eyes were disturbingly clear and alert.

'Before I go, don't you think we should at least exchange names?' he suggested.

'Why?'

His mouth curled into a faintly wicked smile. 'I might want to send you a thank-you letter, for helping me.'

'You can say thank you before you leave,' Nell said shortly.

He kept on smiling, but it was a different kind of smile this time. Something about it made the ends of her nerves tingle in a rather unpleasant way, but she didn't apologise for her rudeness. All she wanted was for him to go and leave her on her own.

'You still haven't told me your name,' he reminded her, making no effort even to stand up, let alone make arrangements to go.

'It's Nell Sutherland,' she muttered—then immediately wished she hadn't told him. After the last couple of weeks, she wanted to spend the rest of her life being completely anonymous!

'Nell Sutherland,' he repeated thoughtfully.

She instantly stiffened. Had he recognised her name? He didn't say anything else, though, and slowly she began to relax again. Surely he would have said straight away if he had known who she was? If he had read any of the garbage that had been printed about her in the Press during the past few days?

It was all right, she told herself with a silent sigh of relief as he continued to say nothing. He obviously hadn't seen the papers, he didn't recognise her face or her name.

'Would you like to know *my* name?' he asked at last.

'Have you remembered it this morning?' she asked, raising one eyebrow. 'Yesterday you didn't seem to have the slightest idea who you were.'

'Yesterday was a very strange day,' he said musingly.

'It certainly was,' she agreed with some feeling. 'And I don't really care if I know your name or not,' she added, still not caring that she was being deliberately rude.

'It's Zack Hilliard,' he told her, ignoring her last remark and her impoliteness.

'Well, Mr Hilliard, since you're obviously feeling much better this morning, I don't think you need to lie around resting any longer. It's time for you to leave,' she told him bluntly.

He made no effort to get to his feet, though. In fact, he relaxed back on the couch, looking very much at home. 'But I like it here,' he said easily.

Nell's expression instantly grew wary. What was he up to now? 'It doesn't matter whether you like it here,' she said, in what she hoped was a firm voice. 'You can't stay.'

'Why not?'

His casual question seemed to hang in the air between them like an invisible challenge. Nell stood very still. Was he being serious? She certainly hoped not!

Of course he hadn't meant it, she told herself edgily. He was just getting his own back because she had been so rude to him. He was enjoying seeing her so discomfited. Well, perhaps she had been a little unreasonable. This might be a good time to change her attitude. Apologise for her rudeness, explain once again—but politely—why he couldn't stay here, then say a friendly goodbye to him, and even wish him well.

'Look,' she said in a much more placatory tone, 'we seem to have got off on the wrong foot this morning, and it's probably mostly my fault. I'm sorry about that. You must realise, though, that I don't much like being in this sort of situation. You know I'm here on my own. Having to take in a perfect stranger makes me feel— well——'

'Vulnerable?' he supplied helpfully.

Nell wasn't at all sure that 'vulnerable' was the right word to describe the way she felt when she was near to this man, but it would have to do for now.

'Yes, vulnerable,' she said firmly. 'I'd have thought you could appreciate that. And be willing to do something about it,' she added pointedly.

His eyes glittered briefly. 'What exactly do you want me to do?'

'You know what I want you to do,' she said with a touch of exasperation. 'I want you to leave. Your memory's come back, and you're obviously feeling very much better this morning. There's no reason for you to stay here any longer.'

'But I've already told you I like it here,' Zack said smoothly.

Nell could feel her temper beginning to stir again. With an effort, she kept it under control. She even managed to keep a friendly note in her voice.

'This is a beautiful part of Tuscany—I can quite understand why you like it. But you have to leave this house.'

'I don't have to do anything,' he told her comfortably.

'Yes, you *do*,' she snapped. Then she stopped herself, took a deep breath, and told herself to be careful. Losing her temper wouldn't be a wise thing to do. He was bigger than her, stronger than her. She had to get out of this situation by using tact and persuasiveness.

She took another steadying breath, then started again. 'I'm asking you to go,' she said in her most reasonable tone of voice. 'I don't want to get into an argument with you, and I certainly don't want to have to call the police and cause a great deal of unpleasantness. So, will you please leave?'

Zack gave a smile that curved the sensual line of his mouth, but never quite reached his eyes.

'I don't think I want to,' he said pleasantly.

Nell's nerves finally began to run riot. It was quite impossible to keep them under control any longer.

'Right, that's it,' she said angrily. 'I've tried being reasonable with you, I've even tried being friendly. I'm just not getting through to you, though, am I?'

'Of course you are,' said Zack in a calm voice. 'You want me out of here, and that's understandable. Unfortunately, I've decided I'm going to stay.'

'You can't stay!' she yelled at him. 'I'm not inviting you to stay!'

'I never asked for an invitation,' he pointed out. 'I simply told you what I intend to do.'

'And I intend that you should go away!'

Nell glared furiously at him, her dark brown eyes boring into his own bright blue gaze. Curiously, she was no longer frightened of him. Perhaps she was simply too angry! she decided. She had tried to help this man, and this was how he repaid her—by abusing her hospitality.

'Perhaps we should talk about this,' Zack suggested.

'There's absolutely nothing to talk about!' she said fiercely.

'Oh, but I think there is,' he said in an unruffled voice. 'You see, there's something that I haven't yet told you. I own this house.'

She gaped at him. 'You—you can't own it!' she spluttered at last.

'Why not?'

'Because—well—because——' she floundered. Then she managed to pull herself together a little. 'I've rented this house for the next two weeks. I made the arrangements through a booking agent, everything's been confirmed in writing. And I know I haven't come to the wrong house.'

'No, you're in the right house,' agreed Zack. 'But it still happens to be *my* house. The booking agent is a friend of mine. Since she only started the business this year, she's been having a few teething problems. She was short of suitable properties, and didn't want to turn away customers in case they didn't come back again, so as a favour I agreed to let her put this house on her books when I'm not using it. It's just a temporary arrangement, until her business gets off the ground.'

Nell looked at him suspiciously. 'Why didn't you tell me all this yesterday, when I brought you back here?' she demanded.

'Yesterday, I couldn't even remember my own name,' he reminded her.

'Are you telling me you didn't recognise your own house when you walked into it?' she challenged him.

'No,' he said calmly. 'As soon as I walked in the door, I realised that everything looked familiar. Then everything slowly began to come back to me, and I realised you'd actually brought me home.'

'But you didn't say anything,' Nell accused.

'No,' he agreed. 'I thought you'd had enough problems to deal with for one day. I decided to let you get a good night's sleep before I sprang any more surprises on you.'

She wasn't sure she believed any of this. 'If you really are the owner, you should have been here to meet me yesterday,' she reminded him.

'The arrangements I'd made were altered at the last moment,' Zack explained in a relaxed voice. 'The reason I was letting the house for a couple of weeks was that I'd arranged to join a few friends on a sailing trip. Then they phoned to say they wanted to sail a day early, so I had to leave earlier than planned. I'd only gone a couple of kilometres, though, when that dog shot out in front of me and I crashed my motorbike, trying to avoid the wretched animal.'

'Then your friends must be worried about you, wondering what's happened to you.'

He shook his head. 'It was a casual arrangement. Anyone who wanted to go along on the trip simply had to get there before the boat sailed. They'll have assumed that I changed my mind at the last moment, since I didn't turn up.'

Nell looked at him warily. Was he telling the truth? On the other hand, what would be the point of lying?

'If you really are the owner of this house, then at least I did the right thing in bringing you here,' she said slowly, at last. 'But now you've recovered from your accident, I expect you want to leave, and carry on with your trip.'

'No point,' said Zack casually. 'The boat will have sailed by now.'

Nell immediately began to feel uneasy again. 'Then what are you going to do for the next couple of weeks?' she asked edgily.

'I've already told you that.' His own voice remained very calm. 'I'm going to stay here.'

'You can't!'

'Of course I can. This is my house.'

'But I've rented it! I've paid in advance.'

'I haven't said you've got to leave.'

'We can't *both* stay here!'

'Why not?' he asked coolly.

Nell realised that this situation was getting completely out of hand. 'Because we don't even know each other,' she burst out. 'I can't spend the next two weeks sharing this farmhouse with a total stranger. Anyway, I came here because I want to be on my own.'

Zack shrugged nonchalantly. 'Unfortunately, we can't always have what we want. But if you're really against the idea of sharing, you can always move out.'

'But I haven't got anywhere else to go!'

'Then you'll have to go back home, to England.'

Just the thought of going back home made Nell shiver. The Press would be waiting for her, and there would be endless phone calls from friends—a lot of whom were turning out not to be friends at all—wanting to know what had really happened. The whole point of coming to this remote farmhouse in Tuscany had been to drop completely out of sight for a while. She hoped that, by the time she did finally go back home, the Press would have latched on to someone else, there would be a new story or a new scandal to divert their attention away from her.

'No, I can't go home,' she muttered at last.

Zack's eyes narrowed. 'Trouble of some kind?'

'No,' she lied defiantly. 'I just—just want to stay here, in Tuscany.'

'Then you'll have to get used to having me around. Don't worry, it won't be a problem. The farmhouse is quite big enough for the two of us—we won't even have to see very much of each other,' he added, his blue eyes gleaming briefly.

'I really don't want to share this place with you,' Nell said stiffly. 'There must be something I can do about this. Perhaps the booking agent can find me another farmhouse?'

Zack immediately shook his head. 'I told you, demand is outstripping supply at the moment—everything she's got is fully booked. I'm sure she'll offer you a full refund, though, in the circumstances.'

'I don't want a refund,' she said a little desperately. 'I want somewhere to *stay* for the next two weeks.'

'I've already told you you can stay here. Be my guest. I realise it isn't an ideal solution for either of us, but we're both adults, I'm sure we can cope with the situation.'

'But I must have some legal rights. I signed an agreement——'

'You probably do have some rights, but by the time you've managed to get in touch with a solicitor and sorted everything out, your two weeks will be up. The way I see it, you've got a straight choice. You can stay here, as my guest, or you can move out.'

Nell didn't like either of those alternatives. Of the two, though, staying here—even as Zack Hilliard's guest— was definitely preferable to going back to England to face the Press. She would do *anything* to avoid that.

'If I stay, I want to pay,' she said finally.

'I don't take money from women,' he told her at once.

'You would have taken your share of the original booking fee,' Nell pointed out.

'That was a business transaction.'

'And this isn't?'

'No. This is my way of saying thank you for stopping and picking me up from the side of the road, when you could so easily have driven past and pretended you didn't even see me.'

'Oh,' she said, blinking a little in surprise. She hadn't looked at it from that point of view before.

'So—are you going to stay?'

Nell tried to look as if she were seriously thinking it over, although she already knew very well what her answer was going to be. This isolated farmhouse was such an ideal place for hiding away from the Press that she would be mad to leave it. And perhaps sharing it with Zack Hilliard wouldn't be such a problem. In fact, she would make very sure it *wasn't* a problem.

'Yes, I'll stay,' she said after a long pause.

'Good.' He smiled. 'It's a long time since I've had a house guest. I'm quite looking forward to it.'

Something in that vivid gaze made her stomach muscles give an unexpected twitch.

'Er—I've still got some unpacking to do,' she said, beginning to back towards the door. 'I think I'd—er—better go up and get on with it.'

A slow grin spread across his face. 'Yes, why don't you do that?'

Was he laughing at her again? Nell decided she didn't want to stay and find out. There was something very unnerving about this man, especially when he relaxed and smiled!

'Yes, I will,' she said hurriedly, and shot out of the door.

Once she was outside, she took a deep breath. Was she mad, agreeing to stay here as Zack Hilliard's guest? Probably! she decided. But this place was the perfect bolt-hole, and she so badly needed to get away from all that relentless intrusion into her private life. She would have agreed to stay just about anywhere, as long as there wasn't a journalist or press photographer in sight!

She went on up to her room and began to unpack, tossing her clothes into cupboards and drawers. Then she realised she was hungry. She hadn't had anything to eat or drink since she had got up this morning.

She left the bedroom and went back down to the kitchen. As she opened the door, though, she stopped dead. There was a handsome older woman bustling around the kitchen, singing happily to herself as she efficiently cleared up a pile of plates and saucepans.

'If you're going to stay here, I'd better introduce you to my housekeeper,' said Zack's voice from just behind her.

Nell immediately jumped several inches into the air. This man certainly had an extraordinary effect on her nerves!

'I've already told you I don't like it when you creep up on me,' she said, much more sharply than she had intended.

'I never creep,' he told her, his blue eyes glinting. 'But, since this is my house, I do go wherever I please. Now, come and say hello to Signora Ginelli. And be nice and polite to her,' he warned softly. 'I don't want to lose the best housekeeper I've ever had.'

Nell was about to protest that she would never do anything to make his housekeeper resign, but Zack was already pushing her further into the kitchen. The dark-haired older woman turned round and gave Zack a big smile. Then she saw Nell, and the smile slowly faded from her face.

'Signora Ginelli, this is Nell Sutherland,' said Zack. 'She's going to be staying here for a couple of weeks.' Then he turned back to Nell. 'Signora Ginelli comes here once a week to clean the house, and to make sure I'm behaving myself. She's looking disappointed at the moment because she's got a very beautiful daughter, Maria, who she thinks I should marry.'

'You would be very happy with Maria,' said Signora Ginelli reproachfully.

'I'm sure I would,' said Zack, grinning at his house-keeper. 'And if I ever decide to marry, then I promise Maria will be at the top of my list. Now, will you show

Nell around, tell her where everything is and explain how things work? I've got to spend the morning trying to find a garage who'll collect and repair my motorbike.'

'You had an accident on your motorbike?' queried Signora Ginelli anxiously. 'That is how you got those cuts and bruises?'

'How else do you think I got them?' Then he gave a grin. 'Or did you think Nell had been beating me up?'

'I'm sure Signorina Sutherland is a very nice girl,' said his housekeeper severely. 'She would never do anything like that.'

'I'm not so sure of that,' said Zack drily. 'Well, I'd better go and make those phone calls. I'll see the two of you later.'

Once he had left the kitchen, Nell felt a little awkward. 'Er—is it all right if I make myself some coffee?' she asked.

'Of course it is,' said Signora Ginelli. She opened a couple of doors, showing Nell a well stocked cupboard. 'You will find everything you need in here.'

'You speak very good English,' remarked Nell, as she rummaged through the cupboard.

'I had an English boyfriend once,' said Signora Ginelli. 'I was young and silly, I thought he was going to marry me, so I made a great effort to learn his language.' She gave a small sigh. 'But he was like Signor Hilliard, very good-looking, very clever at catching ladies—but he didn't want to marry any of them. So I married Signor Ginelli. He's a good man,' she added quickly, 'we are very happy, but——'

'But women always remember their first love?'

'That is the way things are for us,' she nodded. 'Sometimes we remember with happiness, sometimes with sadness. How do you remember it?' she asked Nell.

'I—er—I haven't actually had a first love,' Nell confessed a little reluctantly.

Signora Ginelli immediately looked shocked. 'But you are perhaps twenty-one, twenty-two?'

'Twenty-three,' admitted Nell.

'How did you get to be such an age without falling in love?'

'I suppose I've always been working too hard. You see, I'm an actress—or, at least, *trying* to be an actress. And it's so hard to get parts—you have to keep chasing after readings and auditions, and because you have to live you have to keep taking all kinds of part-time jobs just to pay the rent and eat. I suppose I just haven't had any time to fall in love,' Nell finished defensively.

'There has never been anyone?' asked Signora Ginelli incredulously.

'Well—a little while ago, I thought there might be someone,' Nell said slowly, not even wanting to talk about it. 'But it all turned out very badly, in fact it was a disaster. That's why I've come here, to get away from everything for a while.'

'You think Signor Hilliard will help you to forget? I don't think this is a very good idea,' said Signora Ginelli, with a small frown.

Nell looked at Zack's housekeeper in open-mouthed surprise for a few moments. Then she began to laugh.

'Signor Hilliard and I—we don't even know each other. We hadn't even met, until yesterday.' Then, as Zack's housekeeper looked even more disapproving, Nell added quickly, 'I'm only staying here because of a mix-up. I rented this farmhouse for a couple of weeks, while Mr Hilliard was meant to be away. But because of his accident on his motorbike, he couldn't go, so now we're going to have to share the house for a while. But we've got separate rooms, and that's definitely the way it's going to stay. I don't suppose we'll even be seeing much of each other.'

Signora Ginelli looked relieved. 'That is good,' she said. 'Signor Hilliard is a beautiful man, but he is also very good at breaking hearts. You are obviously a nice girl, I do not think it would be a good idea for you to get involved with him. Anyway,' she added practically, 'I still hope he will one day marry my Maria. She is also very beautiful, so Signor Hilliard would not have time to stray, because he would be too busy making sure that other men did not steal her away from him.'

By this time Nell had made herself some coffee and a sandwich. 'I think I'll have this out on the terrace, in the sunshine,' she said. 'I don't want to get under your feet while you're working.'

'I like having someone to talk to,' said Signora Ginelli comfortably. Then she gave a small frown. 'But I am still not happy about you staying here with Signor Hilliard. It is not right that a young girl should stay alone with a man—people will talk, you will have a bad—a bad——'

'Reputation?' suggested Nell, as Signora Ginelli searched for the right word. She gave a wan smile. 'There's no need to worry about that, I don't really have any reputation left to worry about. But thank you for being concerned. Apart from my parents, you're the first person who's been kind to me for quite some time.'

As Signora Ginelli gave her a puzzled look, Nell grabbed hold of her coffee and sandwich and escaped from the kitchen. She didn't want to talk about herself any more, and she certainly didn't want to answer all the questions that Zack's housekeeper looked as if she wanted to ask.

She went out on to the terrace, slumped into a chair and nibbled unenthusiastically at her sandwich. In front of her stretched the undulating, sunlit Tuscan hills, studded with clusters of olive trees, and the red glow of the terracotta roofs of distant farmhouses. In the distance, rows of vines marched in regimented lines across the hillsides, their grapes slowly ripening in the hot sun. Slowly she began to relax. If any place could help to heal her raw nerves, then this was it. Only she would feel a lot better if she didn't have to share this peace and tranquillity with Zack Hilliard.

Almost as if thinking about him had conjured him up, the door to the farmhouse opened and Zack came out on to the terrace. Nell glanced up at him, and when she saw the icy coldness of his blue eyes and the grim set of his mouth, she instinctively tensed up. What was wrong? Then she relaxed again slightly. It was probably nothing to do with her. Anyway, Signora Ginelli was in the house, and while she was here nothing very awful could happen. Zack's housekeeper didn't seem at all in awe of her rather intimidating employer, and Nell was sure she could count on her support and protection.

'Signora Ginelli has just left,' Zack said shortly, making Nell instantly feel nervous all over again as she realised she was completely on her own with this man. 'But before she went, she found this and asked if I wanted to keep it.'

He tossed a newspaper on to the table. Nell had bought it at the airport, intending to read it on the plane, but in the end she hadn't even bothered to open it.

'It's mine,' she said, with a small frown. 'But I don't want it. You can throw it away, if you want to.'

Zack sat down on the chair opposite her, but, even though he was no longer towering over her, that didn't make him look any less formidable.

'I decided to look through it before I threw it out,' he said softly. His blue gaze slid slowly over her, making her skin break out in an enormous rash of goose-pimples. 'Nell Sutherland,' he went on, in the same dangerously quiet voice. 'When I first heard your name, I thought it sounded familiar. But it wasn't until I saw the item in the gossip column, and the photo that went with it, that everything finally clicked into place. ''The girl who broke a superstar's heart'',' he went on, quoting sarcastically from one of the more florid headlines produced by the popular Press. 'You're famous, Nell—but not for any reasons that you should be proud of.'

Despite the heat of the morning, Nell suddenly felt cold. Her teeth had actually begun to chatter, and she was glad she was sitting down, because she didn't know that her legs would have supported her if she had been standing. 'What did it say about me in the paper this time?' she muttered at last.

'Can't resist your own Press clippings?' said Zack with clear contempt. 'If you really want to know, the Press are interested in why you've suddenly disappeared. It looks as if just about every journalist in Britain wants to find you, to get your side of the story. Clever ploy, Nell,' he went on in a cold voice. 'Disappearing acts always make the headlines. When you do finally sell your side of the story to the gutter Press, it should push up the price very nicely.'

'Do you really think——?' she began in a choked voice.

'Oh, yes, I do think,' he cut in, his blue eyes glinting. 'And don't bother trying to deny it, or producing a few fake tears. You're obviously a good actress, but I'm not interested in seeing one of your performances. And if I'd known who you were from the beginning, I'd have made damned sure you weren't allowed to rent my house.'

Nell rubbed away the brightness from her eyes and felt herself beginning to get very angry.

'How can you say that when you don't know anything about me?' she accused. 'And you don't want to know, do you? It's much easier to believe everything that's been written about me in the papers.'

'I think that, for once, they've got it about right,' Zack returned tautly. 'You chased after Lloyd Kendrick because he's a world-class film star, someone who could boost your career which, up until then, hadn't been going anywhere. When you got him to fall for you—and that probably wasn't too difficult, looking the way you do— you persuaded him to give you a part in his new film. There was a lot of publicity, you were a "hot couple", and you lapped it all up. Once the film was finished, though, and new parts and lucrative offers began to come your way, you decided you didn't need him any more.

So you dumped him. Of course, by then you'd also realised that Lloyd Kendrick's career was on the slide, his last two films had lost money, and you didn't want to be connected to a loser because *you* were on your way up. It didn't matter that he really loved you, or that he fell apart when you walked out. Nell Sutherland is a girl who knows how to take care of number one.'

His damning summary of everything that had been said or written about her in the past couple of weeks momentarily took her breath away. Then she opened her mouth, ready to deny hotly every single word.

In the end, though, she didn't say anything at all. Instead, a stubborn look came over her face. OK, let him believe whatever he wanted to believe, she decided defiantly. No one was interested in hearing her side of the story, no one wanted to know the truth! Well, to hell with all of them! She didn't *care* any more what people thought of her.

'Nothing to say?' Zack challenged her with contempt.

'No,' she got out tightly.

His eyes narrowed. 'I'd like to know exactly what you're doing here. What plans are hatching inside that beautiful and devious little head of yours?'

'I haven't got any plans,' she muttered. Then she shot a sudden defiant look at him. 'I suppose you're going to turn me out, now that you know who I am?'

He gave a low growl. 'I'd certainly like to. But once I've made an agreement, I never go back on it.'

'Then I look forward to being your house guest for the next two weeks,' said Nell, with far more bravado than she had believed she was capable of producing at the moment. 'And I'd just like to say that I really appreciate your high opinion of me,' she added, quickly turning around and walking off as soon as she had finished speaking, because she could feel a warning prickle behind her eyes. And she pretended she couldn't feel Zack's bright blue gaze boring contemptuously into the back of her neck.

I don't care what he thinks of me, I *don't* care, she told herself over and over again, as she walked blindly and aimlessly, wanting only to get away from those accusing blue eyes.

She was beginning to feel as if she could run to the other side of the world, and still not escape from the dark shadow that Lloyd Kendrick had thrown over her life.

CHAPTER THREE

NELL kept on walking, only stopping when she was a safe distance away from the farmhouse. She sat down slowly on the warm grass, her skin glistening damply as the hot sun blazed down on her.

The path she had been following had led her up the hillside behind the farmhouse. From here she could look down on the house below, she could see the tiled roof catching and reflecting the bright sunshine, see the flowers that spilled out of tubs and tumbled over the walls, could see——

Her breath caught abruptly in her throat as she saw Zack walk slowly to the edge of the terrace, then look in her direction, as if he could see her sprawled tiredly on the hot, dry ground. She kept very still, like an animal which remained motionless, trying to hide from the hunter.

She felt her mouth twist into an involuntary grimace. Was that how she thought of him? As a hunter? But she was actually quite safe, she reminded herself. He wasn't interested in her in any way—especially now that he knew who she was. He wasn't even interested in knowing the truth about her.

She gave a deep sigh. No one wanted to know the truth. And she was quite sure no one would believe her if she tried to tell it. The powerful publicity machine behind Lloyd Kendrick had made sure of that.

49

Lloyd Kendrick—Nell remembered how bowled over she had been the first time she had met him. Lloyd had been due to shoot a new film in England, and the production company were holding very well publicised auditions to find an English girl to play opposite him. 'It's obviously a publicity gimmick,' her agent had told Nell. 'They'll probably announce in the end that they can't find anyone suitable, and bring in an American actress. But you might as well go along and read for the part. It'll all be good experience.'

And so Nell had gone along and, to her amazement—and her agent's equal amazement!—she had got the part.

On the first day of shooting, she had been so nervous that she fluffed her lines and shook like a leaf. But Lloyd had been amazingly helpful, his friendliness had got her through those first few awful hours, and at last she had been able to relax and show that she really could act, that they hadn't made a dreadful mistake in choosing her. Then, when the first day's filming was finally over, Lloyd had invited her to dinner—and she had accepted like a shot. To her astonishment, he looked straight into her velvet-brown eyes and told her she was one of the most gorgeous women he had ever seen, and he wanted to spend a lot more time with her.

After that, everything had seemed to take on an almost dreamlike quality. For the next few weeks, when they weren't filming, Nell had gone everywhere with Lloyd. Pictures of them together had soon begun to appear in the Press, who knew a good story when they saw it. 'Famous film star meets unknown actress, and love blossoms overnight...' And they had made an attractive couple, Lloyd with his thick blond hair and sexy smile,

Nell with her long dark hair, big brown eyes, and the kind of bone-structure that photographers fantasised about. The publicity machine had gone into overdrive, and if Nell had just occasionally thought this was a much better advertisement for the film than Lloyd just going on a TV chat show or radio phone-in, and talking about it, or wondered how the Press always knew where they were, turning up in droves at every single place they went to, then she'd pushed those small doubts to the back of her mind and concentrated on enjoying the fun.

And it *had* been fun. Looking back, she was ashamed to admit how much she had liked being the centre of attention. Swept up in the excitement and glamour of it all, she hadn't stopped to think *why* this was happening to her. Or questioned the ever-mounting blaze of publicity that surrounded every single thing that she and Lloyd did.

It was at the end-of-filming party that everything had come crashing down around her. After a couple of hours, Lloyd had disappeared, and, without thinking, Nell went looking for him.

It didn't take her long to find him. Or to realise what he had been about to do to the half-naked girl in his arms.

Totally shocked and hurt, Nell had run straight out and spent the rest of the evening walking aimlessly around the streets of London. By the time she finally returned to her own small flat, she had been too exhausted even to cry. And her last thought, as she slid into a restless, dream-filled sleep, had been that Lloyd's reputation was going to drop to rock bottom when this story finally came out.

Looking back, Nell couldn't believe how naïve she had been, believing that Lloyd would actually tell the Press the true reason for the end of their relationship. What had happened, of course, was that the publicity machine behind him had reacted at once. By next day, the story was all over the papers. A 'broken-hearted' Lloyd had given the best performance of his life as, in a low, dev-astated tone, he had told journalists that his affair with his new leading lady was over; that he had found out, quite by chance, that she was only using him to further her own career. She had never loved him; she had only wanted the fame and publicity that she had got from being romantically linked with him.

The Press lapped up every word of it. Nell was im-mediately branded heartless, a manipulator, and much, much worse. In growing desperation, as her life and her career began to fall apart all around her, she had even tried to get in touch with Lloyd, but she could only get through to his agent, who was callously dismissive.

'Hard luck for you, sweetheart,' he said, 'but very good for my client. Lloyd's career was going downhill, but now you've given him some marvellous publicity and public sympathy's on his side. That's got to be good for Lloyd.'

'Doesn't anyone care what's good for me?' she de-manded, almost in tears.

But it seemed that no one did. And when she tried to argue with Lloyd's agent that destroying her reputation would hardly be good for the film, he simply laughed.

'You've got it all wrong,' he told her. 'Remember, your character in the film walked out on Lloyd in the end. And now you've done exactly the same thing to him in real life. The public will flock to see the film—they'll think they're seeing the real thing.'

A suspicion began to take shape in Nell's mind. 'Was all this planned from the beginning?' she asked slowly.

'Only the fairy-tale love affair between you and Lloyd,' said his agent. Then he chuckled. 'We expected to get some good publicity out of it, but it's turned out even better than we'd hoped for!'

Nell began to feel sick at that point. 'And Lloyd knew about it from the beginning?' she said in a duller voice. 'He agreed to go along with it?'

'Of course he did,' said his agent. 'He'd do anything to revive his career. He just asked us to make sure that the girl we picked to play opposite him was a real good-looker. Lloyd has trouble relating to girls who aren't beautiful. When you waltzed in to that audition, we took one look at you and knew we'd found a real winner.'

She swallowed hard, still feeling nauseated by the way she had been used—and the way she had so stupidly fallen for it.

'What—what if I go to the Press?' she asked in a cracked voice. 'Tell them what *really* happened?'

'Try it,' said the agent, in an unconcerned voice. 'No one will believe you. We got in there first, sweetheart— anything you say now will simply sound like a lot of feeble lies to try and excuse your behaviour.'

And Nell knew he was right. She was just one person up against an expert and efficient publicity machine.

'Sue everyone involved!' her father had said in outrage, when she had rung up in tears and tried to explain what had happened to her bewildered parents.

But Nell hadn't wanted to do that. She couldn't prove her side of the story—Lloyd's agent would certainly never admit to that telephone conversation they had had—and, anyway, it would only have meant more protracted publicity, and she had already had enough of that to last a lifetime. Instead, even while despising herself for her cowardice, she had decided to disappear for a couple of weeks, find somewhere really remote she could hide away. She fervently hoped the Press would forget about her if she wasn't around, that someone else would come along to grab the headlines.

At least she had learned a couple of valuable lessons from the experience, Nell told herself bitterly. The first was that she wasn't in love with Lloyd Kendrick, and knew now that she never had been. She had simply been dazzled by him for a while. And she also knew that she didn't like the person she had become when she was with him. That was one reason why she had wanted these couple of weeks on her own, so that she could try to discover the old Nell Sutherland again. She wanted to be the person she had been before she was bowled over by Lloyd and the dizzying prospect of fame.

She gave a deep sigh, slowly coming back to the present as the hot sun beat down on her unprotected head. She had come to this remote farmhouse in Tuscany to get away from the publicity and the unending attention of the Press, but she was having to share this house with Zack Hilliard, who now knew who she was. So much for her dreams of anonymity!

Of course, she could always move out. But where could she go? Not back to England, where the Press were waiting for her, she decided with a small shudder.

And she couldn't afford to move on and take a room in a hotel. She had had to scrape together every last penny of her savings to pay for these two weeks in Tuscany.

'If you stay out in this sun for too long, you'll get heatstroke,' Zack's voice told her, slightly harshly.

Nell jumped. Wrapped up in her own thoughts, she hadn't heard him approach. He must have moved like a great silent cat, she thought, her nerves giving a small tremor.

'I'm fine,' she said in a low voice. 'Just leave me alone.'

'Not until we've got a few things straight.'

That made her look up at him guardedly. 'What kind of things?'

'I don't know exactly what you're doing here,' he said in the same harsh tone, 'but I want you to understand this. I don't want the Press on my doorstep; I don't want even a single journalist ringing up demanding an interview with you. Is that clearly understood?'

'I came here to get *away* from the Press,' she told him indignantly.

'So you say, but you could be lying. For all I know, this is all part of some new publicity campaign.'

Nell jumped to her feet. 'Are you crazy?' she demanded. 'Don't you think I've had enough publicity to last me a lifetime?'

'That depends on how much you like it,' Zack replied coolly. 'A lot of women thrive on it—they spend their lives chasing after it.'

'Not me!' she said vehemently.

He shrugged. 'I've only got your word for that. But let me give you a warning. If I find that you're here on some sort of publicity gimmick, you'll be very sorry.'

'I came here because it's isolated and it's peaceful, and that's *all*!' Nell snapped furiously.

Zack immediately looked sceptical. 'There are plenty of peaceful places you could go, with the money you earned from the film.'

'I haven't seen a penny of it yet. There's been some trouble with the financing of the film. According to my agent, I'll be lucky if I'm ever paid!'

An even grimmer expression settled over Zack's face. 'Then you've an added incentive for getting every penny you can out of the Press by selling them your story. But don't do it while you're here,' he warned, his eyes fixing on her with a dark intensity. His hand slid round her wrist, holding it in an iron-hard grip that made her realise just how strong this man was. 'Am I getting through to you?'

He certainly was! His face was so close that Nell could feel the warmth of his breath against her cheek. And his vivid eyes bored down into her own, only inches away. She felt as if she could drown in that bright blue gaze.

For several fraught seconds their gazes remained locked together. Then his fingers fractionally increased their grip on her wrist.

'You do understand what I mean when I say no publicity?' he repeated in the same soft voice, and she shivered deeply despite the heat of the sun on her skin.

She somehow managed a short, jerky movement of her head. Zack's grip on her wrist slackened slightly, and his fingertips slid over the smoothness of her skin as if he had suddenly discovered that he liked the touch of her.

His head bent over, and his mouth—that hard, sensual mouth—was so close she could touch it with her own if she leant forward a fraction, just a fraction...

Nell jerked her head away, wrenched her wrist from his grasp, then whipped her entire body away, so that there was no danger that any part of her would touch him.

'Yes, I understand you,' she said in a low, shaken voice. Then she abruptly turned round and ran back down the path that led to the farmhouse. She suddenly had the overwhelming feeling that there was something dangerous here, something that had absolutely nothing to do with the threats Zack had made against her if she ever brought the Press to his house for any reason.

She didn't stop running until she had reached her room, closed the door, and bolted it behind her.

It was quite some time before she at last began to calm down a little. That episode on the hillside had shaken her even more than she had realised.

What exactly happened? she asked herself, running her fingers distractedly through the long, silky strands of her hair. He held your wrist, that was all. And stood closer to you than you liked. So why react like that?

She tried to convince herself that she had simply been frightened of him. A tall, powerful man, looming over her intimidatingly—that was certainly a scary thing to happen.

Yet Nell was honest enough to admit that she hadn't been frightened—at least, not of Zack. It was her own reaction that was making her nerves feel so uncomfortably raw. When he had gripped her tightly and stood only inches away, something inside her had seemed to kick start into life. It had to be body chemistry, she told herself, biting her lip. That strong physical reaction that sometimes flared up between two people who didn't even know each other very well.

Well, for a few seconds her chemistry had certainly gone haywire! When his mouth had hovered close to hers, she had felt a definite tingle in all her nerve-ends. When his vivid blue eyes had locked on to hers, there had been a small, excited jolt in the pit of her stomach.

Nell shook her head despairingly. This was crazy, and she had to put a stop to it *right now*. There just wasn't room in her life at the moment for any more complications.

If it's just a physical reaction, then you can control it, she argued with herself. And if you want to make sure it doesn't happen again, then just don't let him get too close to you. This house is big enough to avoid any close contact with him.

She reminded herself again that she wasn't ready yet for another relationship of any kind. And that she didn't even like Zack Hilliard! After another five minutes of talking to herself in the same vein, she was convinced that she was in control of the situation, and that, now she had recognised what had happened, she would be on her guard in the future and would make sure it never happened again.

With new confidence, Nell unbolted the door and made her way back downstairs. She decided she would have a cup of coffee, then go and do some shopping.

There were a couple of personal items she had forgotten to bring with her when she had packed, and she supposed she ought to buy her own food. She couldn't keep raiding Zack's cupboards.

She had just finished her coffee and was carefully counting the liras stuffed into her purse—she was on a fairly tight budget—when Zack walked into the kitchen.

Nell glanced up at him a little apprehensively, then was relieved to find that she actually felt quite calm inside, her nerves weren't twitching, her stomach wasn't jumping. Whatever had happened to her body chemistry earlier, everything was well under control now.

'I'm going to do some shopping,' she told Zack, getting to her feet.

'There's a small village about three kilometres away; you should be able to get everything you want there. Just keep following the road after it branches to the left.'

She picked up her purse and car keys, and walked towards the door. Then she stopped again when she found that Zack was following her.

'What are you doing?' she demanded, a little more sharply than she had intended.

'I've decided to come with you. I want you to drop me off at the spot where you found me yesterday. Before the garage comes to get my motorbike, I want to collect the luggage I was carrying, and take a look at the bike itself, to see just how much damage was done.'

Nell didn't much like the idea of sharing the car with him, especially since she had only just decided she wanted to keep a safe distance between them. She could hardly refuse to take him, though, so she gave a small grimace and headed out to the car.

She was relieved that Zack didn't want to talk about the confrontation on the hillside. In fact, she had the impression that he had decided to be polite but distant towards her. As he got into the car beside her and they set off, he didn't say another word to her. She was very aware that he didn't actually like her—or, at least, didn't like the person he thought her to be. He had labelled her self-centred, ambitious, greedy for fame and success without caring what she had to do to achieve those things, or whom she hurt.

Nell didn't like any of those labels, but she was also aware that they gave her a great deal of protection against him. He certainly wouldn't want to get involved with anyone who he so thoroughly despised.

It didn't take long to reach the spot where she had found him yesterday. She brought the car to a halt and Zack got out. Then he bent down to speak to her through the window.

'Pick me up on your way back. I'll be waiting here for you.'

It wasn't so much of a request as an order. Nell gave a small scowl and didn't answer him. Then she grated the car into gear and shot off.

She followed the road as it branched round to the left and soon reached the village, which turned out to be a small huddle of shops and houses basking in the hot sunshine. After fishing out her shopping list and phrasebook, she headed towards the general store.

With the help of the phrase-book and a lot of sign language, she managed to buy a bottle of shampoo and some suntan lotion. It took ten minutes, though, and she still had a couple of dozen items on her list!

She was on the point of giving up, because at this rate it would take her the rest of the day to complete her shopping, when the door to the shop opened and Signora Ginelli came in.

'Ah, Signorina Sutherland,' she said, smiling at her. 'Have you come to do some shopping for Signor Hilliard?'

'Certainly not!' answered Nell, a little indignantly. 'He can do his own shopping. I'm trying to buy some things for myself—but I'm not getting very far.'

'If you give me your list, I will help,' offered Signora Ginelli, and Nell gratefully handed it over.

As she and the owner of the shop went through the list quickly and efficiently, Signora Ginelli launched into a flood of Italian, obviously explaining who Nell was and where she was staying. Nell heard 'Signor Hilliard' mentioned a couple of times, and the owner of the shop obviously knew—and liked—him, because he nodded and smiled enthusiastically when Zack's name came up in the conversation.

Nell realised that Zack wasn't just well liked by these people, but that they didn't even consider him an 'outsider'. Signora Ginelli even wanted her daughter to marry him! He must have something more than his good looks going for him that she didn't yet know about.

With her shopping finally completed and paid for, Nell and Signora Ginelli carried it out to the car and loaded it into the boot.

'Thanks for your help,' said Nell with a smile, getting into the car. 'I'd have been there all day if you hadn't turned up, and probably ended up buying all the wrong things!'

'Be careful how you drive, the roads are narrow,' said Signora Ginelli. Then she looked a little worriedly at Nell. 'You will be all right at that house, with Signor Hilliard? If you like, I can come up each day, to make sure that—well, that he is——'

'Behaving himself?' finished Nell with a grin, as Signora Ginelli lapsed into a slightly flustered silence. 'It's all right—Mr Hilliard doesn't even like me, so I'm sure he isn't going to do anything he shouldn't.'

Signora Ginelli looked relieved. 'That is all right, then. Except that you shouldn't be staying with a man at all,' she added more sternly. 'If it gets to be known, then it will ruin your chances of a good marriage.'

'I'm not sure I even want to fall in love, let alone get married,' Nell said in a bleak tone. 'Too many things can go wrong—it never turns out the way you expect.' Then, seeing the puzzled look on Signora Ginelli's face, she went on quickly, 'Don't take any notice of me, I'm just waffling. And please don't worry about me—I can look after myself. Thanks again for your help, and I'll see you next week, when you come up to do the housekeeping.'

She drove away rather hurriedly because she didn't want Signora Ginelli to see that her eyes were suddenly much brighter than they should have been. After all the hard knocks she had taken lately, she had been completely thrown off balance by the older woman's kindness and concern.

Don't cry, she ordered herself sharply. You don't want to have red eyes when you pick up Zack.

She blinked hard several times, and was relieved to feel the tears retreating. As she steered the car along the narrow, winding road, with birds fluttering lazily through the trees and the Tuscan hills shimmering gently in the golden sunshine, she began to feel much better. She had told Signora Ginelli the truth, she said to herself firmly. She *could* look after herself. Life had knocked her flat, but she was going to pick herself up again and fight back. She had had enough of being used and manipulated by other people. From now on, things were going to be different!

She was now very near to the spot where she had first seen Zack yesterday. Had it really been less than twenty-four hours ago? she marvelled. It seemed more like half a lifetime!

She was looking out for him, but it still came as an unexpected shock when she saw him sitting by the side of the road. She remembered how he had looked yesterday, injured and bleeding. A man in need of help. Well, he seemed to have recovered from his accident remarkably quickly! And he certainly didn't need her help and sympathy any more.

As the car drew nearer, Zack stood up. Nell's gaze locked on to him, a tall, powerful man, whose vivid blue eyes were already looking directly back at her, as if silently challenging her.

Nell felt her foot hovering over the accelerator, and for a moment she felt an almost irresistible impulse to drive straight past him. Then she gave a small sigh and brought the car to a halt. She could hardly make a man so recently injured in an accident walk all the way back to the farmhouse.

Zack got into the car, then looked at her levelly. 'You didn't want to stop, did you?'

'No, I didn't,' she admitted in a low voice, rather unnerved by the way he seemed to know exactly what she
had been thinking.

He didn't say another word, but she could feel his
gaze boring into her all the way back to the farmhouse.

They went straight to the kitchen, where Nell began
to make some coffee while Zack sat at the table, still
watching her. That intense blue gaze began to make her
feel nervous.

'What—what would you have done if I *had* driven
right past you?' she asked at last.

'I'd have reminded you that you're a guest in this
house,' Zack said levelly. 'And that I don't tolerate bad
behaviour.'

He stood up and took a couple of steps towards her.
Suddenly nervous, Nell backed away.

'Don't come any closer,' she warned.

'Why not?' His blue eyes locked on to her own wary
brown gaze. 'What on earth do you think I'm going to
do? Hit you?'

'For all I know, you might be going to do exactly that,'
Nell retorted, with far more boldness than she actually
felt.

He growled something under his breath and briefly
looked angry. 'Do you think I'm a violent man?' he
demanded.

'I've no idea. You *could* be. I really don't know that
much about you.'

'If you think I'm capable of knocking you around,
then why are you staying here?'

The answer was very simple, of course. She had only
been reacting edgily to his nearness; she didn't actually

believe a word she had just said. She was absolutely certain he wasn't a man who ever resorted to physical violence. She knew she didn't have any grounds for believing that, but, all the same, she would have staked her life on it.

'I don't think you'd ever hit me,' she admitted at last.

'You're right,' Zack said grimly. 'Although I'm getting to the point where I'm sorely tempted to put you over my knee and spank you.'

'Don't even try it,' Nell warned at once.

A glint of light showed in his eyes. 'Why not?' he said, his voice suddenly sounding much more relaxed. 'Some women like it. They find it—stimulating.'

'Not me,' she said hotly. Then she stared at him suspiciously. 'Now you're laughing at me again, aren't you?' she demanded accusingly.

'You ought to be pleased I haven't entirely lost my sense of humour. Although I wouldn't have found it very amusing if you'd left me sitting by the side of the road. Perhaps you ought to apologise for even thinking about it?'

'I'm not going to apologise for anything,' Nell told him stubbornly. 'In fact, *you're* the one who should be apologising. You agreed to rent me this house, but nothing's turned out the way I expected. In fact, my entire holiday's been ruined.'

'Like you, I don't intend to apologise for anything,' Zack said smoothly. 'I'm rarely in the mood for apologies of any kind.' Then a brighter light began to glow in his eyes, so that the vivid blue became more intense. 'But I'm beginning to think there is something I'm in the mood for,' he said more softly, and took a step towards her.

Nell felt her nerves give a hefty twitch. Then, as those deep blue eyes bored even more deeply into her own, she felt a warm glow in the pit of her stomach, a glow that grew hotter as Zack took yet another step forward.

Oh, no, she thought with rising panic. It was the body chemistry again! She had thought she had it well under control, but now it was threatening to get out of hand, and she suddenly knew she had to *do* something.

With a muffled yelp of alarm, she turned round and fled.

Three steps led from the kitchen to the terrace outside. Nell went crashing down them, quite literally. The world cartwheeled around her, then she landed on the uneven flagstones with a thump that knocked the breath right out of her.

For a few moments everything went alarmingly dark. Then the world slowly swam back into focus, and she saw Zack bending over her, frowning now, and his blue eyes looking unexpectedly concerned.

'Lie still,' he ordered. 'Get your breath back, then tell me what hurts.'

'Everything hurts,' she complained in a shaky voice. Then her eyes flew wide open as she felt his hands running over her. 'What are you doing?' she demanded in alarm.

'Checking to see if anything's badly damaged,' he said briefly.

'It isn't,' she said with far more conviction than she felt. She struggled to sit up, groaning as her bruised bones protested.

'Did you knock your head?' he asked.

'No. Although I think I bashed just about everything else! Will you stop *touching* me?' she added crossly, as his fingers ran down her legs and encircled one of her ankles, leaving small and yet not unpleasant trails of goose-pimples in their wake.

'You've sprained your ankle,' he told her. 'It's already slightly swollen. Apart from that, you're just bruised. I'll put a bandage round that ankle, though, until we can get it professionally strapped up. It'll make it a little easier to walk on it.'

He went back into the farmhouse, while Nell sat on the terrace, absolutely furious at this latest turn of events. One calamity just seemed to be following after another. And, unlike the others, this latest one really wasn't her fault. After all, she couldn't be blamed for trying to get away from Zack, could she? Especially when that predatory glint had appeared in his eyes! If only she had looked where she was going when she had bolted. Now she was in an even worse mess, hobbling around on one leg!

Zack returned fairly quickly, with a roll of bandage from the first-aid kit in the bathroom. He neatly strapped up her ankle, then deftly tied the ends of the bandage.

'You've made a good job of that,' Nell conceded reluctantly.

'I'm competent at a lot of things,' he said, his eyes gleaming.

Nell decided she didn't want to know what other things he was competent at! She got stiffly to her feet, but then gave a small yelp as she tried to put her injured ankle to the ground.

'Want me to carry you into the house?' offered Zack.

'No, thank you,' she said through gritted teeth. She was absolutely determined to hang on to some shreds of her independence.

Her ankle would just about take her weight, and she hobbled slowly into the kitchen and thankfully collapsed on to a chair.

'A hot bath would help to ease the bruises,' Zack told her, following her inside. 'Want me to run some water for you?' he added helpfully.

'I can do it myself, thank you,' Nell told him in a stilted voice.

'Do you always refuse all offers of help?' he asked, looking at her consideringly.

'I'm quite capable of looking after myself.' That was such a long way from the truth, though, that Nell didn't know how she had the nerve to lie so brazenly.

Zack's gaze locked on to her thoughtfully. 'If you're so good at looking after yourself, why did you make such a mess of that publicity campaign you planned around your affair with Lloyd Kendrick?' he asked at last.

'I did not——' she began fiercely. Then she promptly shut up. She had already decided she didn't have to—didn't *want* to—explain anything to this man. 'That isn't any of your business,' she said in a much lower voice.

Zack immediately hooked one finger under her chin, forcing her head up so that she had to look directly into his eyes. They were vividly alight, as if lit by an inner glow.

'While you're in my house, everything you do is my business,' he told her softly. 'Remember that.' Then, to her utter relief, he let go of her again. 'I'll go and run the water for your bath,' he said in a more normal tone.

As he left the room, Nell sat there gently shaking as she remembered the force of that blue gaze as it had blazed down into her own apprehensive brown eyes. And the quivering, involuntary response of her own nerve-ends.

CHAPTER FOUR

NELL half hobbled, half hopped out of the kitchen, managing to get as far as the sitting-room, where she collapsed on to the couch and sat in a small, aching huddle. And it wasn't only her body that hurt. Even her spirit felt bruised.

This farmhouse wasn't the quiet retreat she had hoped it would be. Instead, it was turning into a positive minefield! And she couldn't even run away. For at least the next couple of days, she wasn't going to be able to do much more than hop for a few painful steps.

The door opened and Zack came in. 'Your bath's ready,' he told her.

'I want to see a doctor first,' she said firmly. She didn't like being immobile, it put her at too much of a disadvantage.

To her surprise, he didn't argue with her. 'I'll go and ring for an appointment,' he said.

He was back in just a couple of minutes. 'The doctor can see you right now. Get yourself into the car, and I'll drive you there.'

Nell hopped out to the car, then gave a small sigh of relief as she sank on to the front seat. Less than ten minutes later, Zack pulled up outside a small house slightly set back from the road. Nell hauled herself out of the car, but when Zack went to take her arm and help her inside, she shook herself free of him.

'Thank you, but I can manage on my own,' she said firmly. It was about time she took charge of her life again, and she could begin by dealing with this latest catastrophe by herself.

'You might not need me to help you into the house, but you're going to need someone to translate for you,' Zack said coolly.

Nell gave a faint groan. 'The doctor doesn't speak English?'

'Why should he? His patients are all Italian.'

So much for her decision to be independent! Nell hobbled into the house, and then had to listen to the doctor and Zack conversing at some length in fluent Italian. Then the doctor, a competent-looking older man, ran his fingers over her ankle, gently prodding and carefully moving her foot around as he assessed the damage.

As he examined her, he directed more questions at Zack who, after a short pause, answered at some length. The doctor's eyebrows rose gently, then he smiled. Nell looked at the two men suspiciously. What was going on here?

'What's he asking?' she demanded of Zack.

'He simply wanted to know how you injured your ankle. I explained that you fell down some steps,' Zack said smoothly.

Nell was absolutely sure Zack had said a great deal more than that. Then the doctor said something more to Zack, and at the same time gave him the kind of smile that one man often gave another when they were sharing a private joke.

'*Now* what's he saying?' she asked suspiciously.

'He's simply commenting that I'm very lucky to have such a beautiful house guest.'

And Nell could guess how the doctor interpreted 'house guest'!

'I don't want him to think——' she began indignantly. 'Look, I want you to explain to him who I am, and why I'm staying with you!'

'No, I don't think I want to do that,' Zack said softly. The line of his mouth had changed and become less relaxed. 'I don't particularly want anyone to know too much about you, or why you're here. Why advertise to the world that Nell Sutherland is staying under my roof? The more people who know about it, the more likely it is that that piece of information will eventually reach the Press. And if I ever open my door one day and find a journalist standing there——'

That half-finished threat stopped Nell in her tracks. Then her shoulders slumped. Was all that bad publicity going to follow her around and haunt her for the rest of her life? she wondered dully.

The doctor looked up at her, gave a faint frown, then spoke rapidly to Zack, obviously asking more questions. Another long conversation followed, but Zack's answers seemed to satisfy the doctor, because he slowly relaxed again before issuing what was clearly a list of instructions.

'He says there isn't any serious damage to your ankle,' Zack translated, 'but you're to keep it bandaged for at least another couple of days, and walk on it as little as possible. He stresses that it's particularly important to rest it. He'll give you a couple of painkillers in case it aches at night, and keeps you awake.'

'Thank you,' muttered Nell, looking up at the doctor. He smiled back at her, then looked rather enviously at Zack. It was clear that he still believed Nell was a lot more than simply Zack's house guest!

She didn't have enough energy to try and convince him otherwise. Anyway, Zack would have to translate for her, and she wouldn't even know if he was giving the doctor a truthful version of what she was saying.

They drove back to the farmhouse in silence. Once they were inside, Zack moved towards the stairs.

'I'll go and run you some fresh bath water,' he said.

'You don't have to wait on me,' Nell said stiffly.

'It rather looks as if I do,' he said drily. 'The doctor's instructions were fairly explicit. You're to do as little as possible for the next couple of days.'

But Nell didn't like the idea of being reliant on this man. 'I can look after myself,' she insisted. 'Please go away and let me cope with this on my own.'

'There's no point in being difficult or childish about it,' Zack said, his tone beginning to sound rather less relaxed.

'Childish?' she repeated with sudden fierceness. 'Well, I don't happen to think it's childish to turn down help from someone who makes you fall down a flight of steps!'

Small, warning lines began to appear at the corners of Zack's mouth. 'I didn't make you fall down that flight of steps.'

'You didn't actually push me. But you were going to——' Nell broke off abruptly, because she didn't want to finish that particular sentence. It would mean telling

him she had turned and run because she had thought he
was going to kiss her. And perhaps go even further.

'What was I going to do, Nell?' he challenged, looking
straight at her. 'Or what did you *think* I was going to
do?' When she didn't answer him, his blue eyes narrowed. 'It's all inside your head—you're over-
dramatising the whole thing. When you've had your bath
and rested, perhaps you'll be more prepared to be
reasonable about the situation.'

He went upstairs, and a few seconds later she could
hear hot water running in the bathroom. Was she being
unreasonable? Probably, she decided. But she had the
feeling that she could take a dozen baths and rest for a
week, and still not feel any better about the prospect of
Zack Hilliard looking after her for the next couple of
days.

She sat at the bottom of the stairs because, quite suddenly, she felt too tired to hobble any further. A few
minutes later Zack came back down and stood in front
of her.

'Your bath's ready,' he told her.

She got to her feet, but as soon as she started to put
a little weight on her painful ankle, it gave way and she
fell over.

Somehow, sprawling on the floor in front of him was
the last straw. She could feel tears prickling hotly at the
back of her eyes, and had to fight fiercely to control
them. She was *not* going to cry in front of this man!

Zack looked down at her for a few moments. Then
he gave a small sound of exasperation, bent down and
scooped her up.

'What are you doing?' she gulped.

'Taking you upstairs to the bathroom,' he told her, heading towards the door.

'I don't need your help,' she insisted, beginning to wriggle and squirm, trying to make him let go of her.

'Of course you need my help,' he told her calmly. 'The only other way you're going to get upstairs is by crawling up on your hands and knees. And that's even more un- dignified than being carried up, don't you think?'

'I could make it on my own!'

'I'm beginning to think there are very few things you can do on your own. And if you don't stop wriggling, I'll probably drop you, and there's every possibility you'll injure your ankle.'

Nell stopped moving, because she could see that made sense. She didn't say anything else, either, subsiding into what she hoped was a dignified silence. Although it was very hard to be dignified when you were being carried like a baby!

When they reached the bathroom, Zack put her down. Then he looked at her, and his eyes glinted.

'Not going to thank me for carrying you up here?'

'I don't think I'm in the mood to thank you for any- thing,' said Nell, careful to keep her tone polite so that he couldn't accuse her of rudeness. 'Now, would you please leave? I want to take my bath.'

'You don't need any—help?' he suggested delicately.

That made her own brown eyes glow hotly. 'No, I don't!'

'Pity,' he murmured regretfully. 'But if you really want to bath on your own, then don't lock the door. If you fall and knock yourself out, I won't be able to help you.'

With that, he turned round and left the bathroom. Nell let out a huge sigh of relief. Living with Zack Hilliard was getting to be a real strain. She was never sure what he was going to say—or do.

She certainly hadn't expected that he would carry her upstairs! That hadn't been necessary, she told herself fiercely, conveniently ignoring the fact that she had only one good leg at the moment. It had been so easy for him to override her protests, though. His arms had gripped her so tightly that all the wriggling in the world wouldn't have freed her.

She gave a small shiver as she remembered the strength in those arms. She wasn't a tall girl, and she was delicately built, but, even if she had been a strapping great Amazon, she would have been no match for him in strength.

Still shivering slightly, Nell twisted her long dark hair up on top of her head and secured it, then began to strip off her clothes. She was down to her lace-trimmed bra and panties when she realised that the bathroom door was still ajar. Hurriedly, she closed it. Then, ignoring Zack's last instruction, she also locked it.

The bath water was still piping hot, and she gave a small sigh of pleasure as she took off her undies and lowered herself into it, carefully resting her bandaged ankle out of the water. She tipped in a generous measure of bath foam, then lazily swirled the water until she was surrounded by tiny bubbles. Then she lay back and felt her aches and pains gently begin to float away.

After a quarter of an hour, the water began to cool. Nell was reluctant to get out, though. This was the most relaxed that she had felt for days. She topped up the bath with more hot water, frothed up the foam again, then settled back and closed her eyes.

A few minutes later she slid into a light doze. Then she fell more deeply asleep. She didn't hear the light tap on the door, didn't hear Zack call her name, quietly at first, and then with growing concern. She didn't even hear when he thumped more loudly on the door.

She *did* hear the crash as he kicked the door in, though. As the lock splintered loudly, every nerve in her body jumped and her eyes flew wide open.

For a couple of seconds she couldn't figure what was going on. She blinked dazedly a couple of times. Then she realised she was still lying in the bath—with most of the covering film of bubbles having long since vanished!—and Zack was looming over her, staring right down at her.

'What the hell do you think you're doing?' she yelled at him, her heart still pounding crazily from the shock of being woken up so rudely and abruptly. Then she realised that just about every inch of her was on view to those all-seeing blue eyes. She grabbed a sponge, but it was too small to cover up anything useful. She tossed it away, and lunged for the towel that was draped over the rail near to the bath. As soon as she began to put her weight on her ankle, though, it gave way, and she slithered back into the bath. Water sloshed everywhere, and she let out a howl of anger and frustration.

Zack looked down at her fiercely. 'I told you not to lock the door!'

Nell glared straight back at him. 'I don't care what you told me. I wanted some privacy, and the only way to get it was to lock you out. Or *try* to lock you out.'

Then she realised that his eyes were no longer fixed so rigidly on her face. Almost reluctantly, they seemed to be moving down, to be taking note of the sleek shape of her body beneath the sloshing water. 'Give me that towel,' she said through gritted teeth.

'I don't like bad manners,' he drawled, his eyes glinting. 'First of all, you say please.'

'I don't have to be polite to you!'

Zack lifted the towel from the rack and held it away from her, so she had no hope of grabbing hold of it.

'I rather think you do,' he said softly.

Nell didn't know which was worse, having to give in to this man or remaining stark naked in front of him. Then a fresh gleam in his vivid blue eyes helped her to make a hurried decision. With a huge gulp, she swallowed her pride.

'Please give me that towel,' she said in a stiff voice.

'See how easy it is when you try?' said Zack with a cool smile. Then he handed her the towel.

Nell immediately draped it round her, not caring that it was dangling in the water and getting soaking wet. 'Why did you kick in the door?' she demanded.

'I knocked, and called your name, but you didn't answer. I thought you might have passed out.'

'Well, I hadn't!'

'Obviously not,' he said more drily. 'But don't you think you should thank me for being concerned for your welfare?'

'I don't want to thank you for anything,' Nell said ungratefully. 'And especially not for leering at me while I'm in the bath!' she added, clutching the towel even more tightly.

'Was I leering?' he said in a surprisingly equable voice. 'I thought I was simply admiring what's an amazingly good body.'

To Nell's absolute irritation, she felt a wave of colour begin to sweep across her face. Don't blush, *don't* blush, she instructed herself furiously. Don't let this man know his remarks can get to you in any way.

'By the way, did you know your towel is beginning to float away?' Zack went on helpfully.

Nell grabbed at it. 'Get out of here! I want to get dressed,' she said tensely. Then she remembered what he had said earlier, and took a deep breath before forcing out the next words. '*Please* get out of here,' she said, hating to have to say that word to him.

'Good girl,' he said approvingly. 'By the time you finally leave here, you may have learnt how to be polite to people.'

'I'm perfectly polite to most people,' Nell told him, shooting a filthy look at him. 'But at times, it's very hard having to be polite to you!'

'But you'll make the effort, won't you?' he said pointedly. 'Because this is my house. And because that's the way I like it.'

'I suppose you think you can lay down all these rules just because you're bigger than I am, stronger than I am,' she challenged him recklessly.

Zack's face changed, and a dark growl of pure exasperation sounded in his throat. He strode towards the bath, ignoring the fact that Nell immediately abandoned her show of bravado and shrank back nervously as he loomed over her.

'If I wanted to throw my weight around, do you know what I'd do?' he said tightly. He reached into the bath and yanked her out, ignoring that fact that she was dripping water all over himself and the floor. 'I'd ignore all your protests, I wouldn't even bother to argue with you,' he told her, gripping her firmly and striding out of the bathroom. 'Nor would I give you any choices. I'd only do what *I* wanted to do.' They had reached the door of her bedroom now, and Nell gave a loud, audible gulp. Zack heard it, and gave a grim smile of satisfaction. 'Are you getting the message?'

She certainly was. And she didn't like it!

He tossed her on to the bed. The wet towel flapped loose and she grabbed it, then held on to it as if it were some kind of safety line.

Zack leant over her, his hand resting against the towel, and she could feel the heat of his palm burning right through its wetness to her skin.

'Because I'm stronger than you, there are a great many things I could do now—if I chose,' he said softly.

Nell's heart thumped so hard and fast that she could hardly breathe, but the worst thing was that it wasn't thumping because she was frightened, but because she was excited! She could feel her skin quivering where his palm burnt against it, there was a queer hot ache in the pit of her stomach, and all her nerve-ends felt raw.

Body chemistry, she told herself, thoroughly shaken. That's all it is—body chemistry! Just remember that and you'll be all right, you'll be able to cope with this.

His vivid blue eyes bored down into hers. His hand moved a fraction so that the tips of his fingers touched the outer swell of her breast, yet even that contact was electrifying. Nell had to bite back hard a small moan.

There was a trace of colour in Zack's own face, and his breathing wasn't quite so steady. For what seemed like half a lifetime, they stared at each other, blue gaze locked on to brown. Then, with a visible effort, Zack eased himself away from her.

'Don't ever again accuse me of using my strength against you to get what I want,' he warned softly. 'If I'd ever had any intention of doing that, then I would have done it just now.'

She could still feel the heat pulsing from him. Or was it from her?

'You look flushed, Nell,' he went on in that same soft voice. 'Are you sorry I won't force you to take this further? But if you want me to, you'll have to ask.'

And the awful thing was that she was tempted! The silken sound of his voice, his musky scent, the heat of his body—they all seemed to be having a catastrophic effect on her own nervous system.

Body chemistry, warned the small voice inside her head again. It's so dangerous; it can lead you astray. Don't let it happen!

Nell dragged in a deep breath and somehow managed to get control over her rioting emotions.

'You don't think I'd ever ask you to touch me?' she demanded in a stilted voice that didn't sound in the least like her own.

Zack moved further away from her. 'No, I don't think you would,' he agreed, his voice suddenly becoming much more hostile. 'You don't embark on an affair unless you think it's going to further your career, do you?'

She wasn't prepared for the raw hurt that his words dredged up from deep inside her. It doesn't *matter* what this man thinks of you, how low an opinion he has of you, she told herself desperately. She couldn't quite seem to convince herself, though.

'Do you think——?' she got out in a choked voice. Then she managed to get a little control over herself. 'Do you really think I'm the kind of person who only gets into bed with someone if I can get some publicity out of it?'

'According to the newspapers, that's exactly the kind of person you are,' Zack replied flatly. 'Or was Lloyd Kendrick lying?'

Yes, she longed to say. She wasn't guilty of anything, except perhaps being too gullible and naïve. At the last moment, though, she stopped herself. Why should Zack Hilliard believe her, when no one else would?

'Why did you suddenly throw Lloyd Kendrick's name at me?' she asked in a much duller voice.

Zack's face hardened. 'Because when I look at you, I see him. I see him kissing you, touching you——' He broke off abruptly, as if he had only just realised what he was saying. He growled something under his breath, swung round and strode towards the door. When he reached it, though, he turned back and stared at her. 'Innocent? Or an ambitious little bitch who'll use anyone to get what you want?' His gaze raked over her as she lay sprawled on the bed where he had left her. 'You're the only one who knows, Nell. And you're not telling anyone, are you?'

He left the room, slamming the door behind him. Nell lay there in a daze. He had behaved like a man who was jealous, she realised in amazement. But that was impossible! She had to be wrong about that.

She thought about it again, able to be a little more calm and rational now that Zack had gone, and finally decided that she definitely *was* wrong. Whatever had caused that outburst, it couldn't possibly have been jealousy.

She lay back on the bed and let out a rather ragged sigh. This was all getting completely out of hand, and, the trouble was, there didn't seem to be anything she could do about it. And with her injured ankle, she was at an even bigger disadvantage.

But what would she do if her ankle weren't injured? Tell herself she hated Zack, pack her things and leave? Nell gave an even deeper sigh. But she certainly hadn't hated him a few minutes ago, when he had been leaning over her, every inch of his hot, hard body causing chaos inside her simply by being near to her. What would have happened if he had taken it further? If he had slid that powerful body even closer, so that it had touched her from head to toe?

A deep shiver went right through her, making even her teeth chatter. What was wrong with her? How could she have such a strong physical reaction to a man she barely knew? She had to put a stop to it right now, before it led to another great disaster. She just couldn't cope with another turbulent upheaval in her life.

Nell spent the rest of the day trying to convince herself that everything was fine, that she could cope with this— could cope with Zack. It was made a lot harder by the fact that Zack was around for so much of the time, bringing her drinks, a meal, anything she needed, since he wouldn't allow her to put her injured foot to the ground. To her relief, he didn't say a word about what had happened upstairs. Perhaps, like her, he just wanted to forget it!

With the help of a couple of aspirins, she managed to get a few hours of sleep that night. In the morning, she was woken up by the sun shining warmly into her room. She opened her eyes, and for a couple of seconds almost felt good about life as she gave a lazy stretch. As soon as she moved, though, her ankle gave a sharp twinge and all her bruises began to ache.

'Great,' she muttered. 'I'm a physical wreck, as well as a mental one!'

She bathed and dressed slowly, then hopped down to the kitchen. She squeezed some fresh orange juice into a glass, and went out on to the terrace to drink it in the warm sunshine.

Zack was already out there, sprawled comfortably on the sunlounger. As usual, he was casually dressed in jeans and an open-necked shirt, and he looked very relaxed.

'How are the injuries this morning?' he asked, his blue gaze sliding slowly over her, down to her still swollen ankle.

'I'll survive,' she said, sitting down at the table. 'Actually, I can put a little weight on my ankle this morning.'

'Just make sure you don't overdo it.' Then his blue gaze rested thoughtfully on her face. 'I think there are one or two things we need to talk about,' he said at last.

Nell was immediately on her guard. 'What kind of thing?' she asked warily.

'Yesterday, things got—rather out of hand. It would be better for both of us if that didn't happen again.'

'It certainly would,' she agreed at once. 'I can do without problems like that!'

His blue eyes focused on her more intensely. 'Then yesterday *was* a problem for you?'

She was about to say that it certainly had been, but then suddenly stopped herself. She definitely didn't want him to know that being physically close to him was getting to be a big problem! And it wasn't, she told herself stubbornly. She just had to control her stupid body chemistry; if she could do that, everything would be fine.

In the meantime, she had to convince him that yesterday hadn't meant anything to her at all.

'I don't have any problems I can't cope with,' she said with far more conviction than she felt.

'Aren't you a lucky girl?' Zack mocked her gently. 'There are a lot of people who'd love to be able to say that.'

'Including you?' she said, without thinking. 'What possible problems could you have?'

'Until a couple of days ago, I didn't think I had any at all,' he said drily. Then he got to his feet. 'I'm going to borrow your car,' he told her. 'There are a few things I need to get from the village, and I want to check on the repairs to my bike. Is there anything you want me to get for you?'

'Oh, you know me,' retorted Nell with a touch of sarcasm. 'I'm the girl who'll do anything for publicity and fame. Just bring me the local journalist, so I can give him a story that'll really jump off hot from the presses.'

Zack shot a long, hard look at her. 'If you put on that act with other people, as well as with me, then it's hardly surprising that everyone's got such a low opinion of you,' he said levelly. And while the colour was still rising in Nell's face, he collected the car keys and left the house.

After he had gone, she stared into the distance for quite some time, preoccupied with her own very private thoughts. Then she gave a small sigh, mentally shook herself, hauled herself to her feet and hobbled into the house. She hadn't had breakfast yet, and she thought it would be a good idea to eat it now, while Zack was out of the house. Her appetite seemed to vanish whenever he was around!

When she had eaten and cleared away the dishes, she hopped back out on to the terrace and stretched out on the sunlounger. The soft cushions still bore the imprint of Zack's body, though, and for some reason that disturbed her. She plumped them up until they looked fresh and untouched, then settled down again.

The golden sunshine blazed down, and the hills all around shimmered gently in the heat. The scent of flowers drifted gently on the air, and the only sound came from the birds in the trees behind the farmhouse.

Nell felt her bruised, aching body slowly relax, and after a while she dozed. After about an hour she woke up again, still feeling the welcome lack of tension.

This was how it *should* be, she told herself. No hassle, no tension—no Zack. If only she could have had a couple of weeks of this peaceful solitude, she would have felt more than ready to face the world again.

Then she sighed. It was no use indulging in wishful thinking. She was here as Zack's house guest, and that situation wasn't going to change. She just had to cope with the situation as it was.

She closed her eyes again, intending to go back to sleep. She wanted to make the most of this tranquil time on her own. Just a couple of minutes later, though, she heard the sound of the car pulling up outside.

Her nerves gave a familiar twitch. As always, they were over-reacting to the thought of seeing Zack again.

He came straight back out on to the terrace. 'Have you been all right while I've been away?'

'Oh, I think I've just about managed to cope,' she said drily. 'Anyway, you weren't gone for very long.'

'Just long enough to buy what I needed,' he told her easily. 'Although it looks as if the repairs to my bike are going to take some time. They need a couple of new parts, and they're going to have to send away for them. The local garage has a fairly limited stock of spares.'

'Then why not use a garage that's better equipped?'

'Because the local people need the work. I think, if you live in a small community, you should support it in every way you can.'

'If you take that kind of attitude, I suppose it's why people around here seem to like you,' remarked Nell.

'Quite a few people like me,' he assured her equably. 'Although I'm not at all sure that includes you.'

'Why wouldn't I like you?' she countered warily.

His blue eyes glittered. 'I'm sure you have your reasons. Although, sometimes, I think I could make you like me very much,' he went on, his voice gradually dropping to a low purr.

Nell instantly hauled herself to her feet, putting all her weight on her good leg. 'I don't either like or dislike you,' she declared, fervently hoping she was sounding convincing. 'You're just someone I'm sharing this house with for a couple of weeks.'

His gaze remained locked on her own wary brown eyes, and amusement gleamed in the impossibly vivid blue depths. 'Am I?' he challenged her softly.

Goose-pimples suddenly crawled over her skin, despite the heat of the sun beating down on her. There was something so very—*physical* about this man, she realised with an inward shiver. And something else, something even more dangerous, that wasn't physical at all.

She forced herself to ignore the suddenly electric atmosphere that seemed to hum between them.

'I don't think we ought to be having this kind of conversation,' she told him in a jerky voice. 'It isn't—sensible. Not in the circumstances.'

'And what circumstances are those?' he enquired softly.

Nell could feel her face becoming flushed. What was he up to now? What was he trying to make her say? Her confusion seemed to amuse him still further, because his mouth began to curl into a smile.

'I don't see what you're grinning at,' she said fiercely.

'Of course you don't,' he said with an even bigger grin. 'But that's because you can't see how funny you look, standing there on one leg, getting very red-faced and indignant.'

'I am indignant!' she told him angrily.

'Then it's rather a shame you can't stalk out and make an impressive exit,' he said sympathetically. 'It's really going to ruin the whole effect, Nell, when you hop away.'

She had to grit her teeth to stop herself saying something very, *very* rude. Then she turned round and hobbled back into the house with as much dignity as she could, under the circumstances.

She had the feeling that few people came out best in an encounter with Zack Hilliard. But she promised herself that, one day, she would be one of them.

CHAPTER FIVE

NELL retreated to her room for a while, limping with difficulty up the stairs. Soon, though, she got bored with sitting and looking out of the window. The view over the sunlit Tuscan hills was magnificent, but even the most captivating view began to pall if you looked at it for too long.

She tried reading a paperback she had brought with her, then began to listen to a tape on her personal stereo, but she couldn't seem to concentrate on either the words or the music. There was too much going on inside her head. She longed to go for a long walk, because fresh air and exercise always helped her to think straight, but that was out of the question at the moment. In the end, she hopped back downstairs to the sitting-room. There was no sign of Zack, and she was rather alarmed at how disappointed that made her feel. You don't want to see him, she told herself firmly. You really *don't*.

She looked around, trying to find something that would stop her from thinking about Zack. There was a newspaper lying on the table, and she realised he must have brought it back with him that morning. She picked it up, but then wrinkled her nose. It was in Italian! That was all right for Zack, who spoke it fluently, but she couldn't understand a word of it.

All the same, she began to flick idly through the pages, simply because there wasn't anything else to do. Then she became very still, because she suddenly found herself staring at a small photograph of a very familiar face.

Zack's picture—here, in an Italian newspaper! Her heart gave an unexpected thump. What was this all about?

Then her gaze slid to the name printed under the photo. It said 'Jackson Paine'.

'Jackson Paine?' she repeated out loud, in bewilderment. For just a moment the name seemed vaguely familiar, as if she had heard it before. The photo was definitely of Zack, though. Even in slightly blurred black and white, there was no mistaking his distinctive eyes, the forceful line of his jaw and the strong, sensual curve of his mouth. What the hell was going on here?

Nell pored over the article underneath with growing frustration. Apart from a couple of basic words, she couldn't translate any of it. One short phrase stood out, though: '*Un milione*'—did that mean a million? she wondered. But a million of what?

She was still trying to figure it out when the newspaper was suddenly whipped away from her. She gave a nervous gulp and turned round, to find Zack standing behind her, holding the newspaper and not looking particularly pleased.

It really was unnerving, the way such a powerfully built man could move so silently. Then she remembered what she had seen in the paper, and looked up at him with a suspicious frown.

'Your picture's in that newspaper,' she told him.

'Is it?' He flicked through to the right page, and glanced at the article. 'Not a very good photo,' he commented.

'But it *is* you. It doesn't say "Zack Hilliard" underneath, though,' Nell said challengingly. 'It says "Jackson Paine".'

'Yes, it does,' agreed Zack, in a cool and uninterested tone.

'Well, I think I'd like an explanation!'

'I don't intend to give you one. As far as I'm concerned, it's none of your business.'

'It certainly is!' retorted Nell with some indignation. 'I'd like to know exactly who I'm sharing this house with, Zack Hilliard or Jackson Paine.'

'The fact that you're here as my guest for a couple of weeks doesn't give you the right to pry into my private life,' Zack told her rather more tersely.

'I still want an explanation,' she insisted.

'You're not going to get one. And if you don't like the situation, remember you're under no obligation to stay here.'

Before she could argue with him any further, he turned round and strode out of the room. If her ankle had been better, Nell might have gone after him, in a determined effort to get more information out of him. She felt at a distinct disadvantage, though, only being able to hobble and hop. And since she didn't like feeling at a disadvantage where Zack was concerned, she stayed where she was and brooded over this unexpected discovery.

All sorts of wild theories flitted through her head, but none of them produced an acceptable reason why Zack should be known by another name. She was highly disturbed by this piece of information she had unearthed. Just who was she sharing this house with?

Rather belatedly, she realised just how little she knew about Zack Hilliard—or was he Jackson Paine? She didn't know where he came from, what he did, or why he was living here in this remote corner of Tuscany. In fact, as she thought about all these things in depth for the first time, she slowly realised that it really wasn't at all sensible for her to have agreed to stay here with someone she knew so little about. Why hadn't she asked more questions from the very beginning? She supposed she had been lulled into a false sense of security by the fact that he was obviously known by the local people— and even liked. And, of course, she had assumed that the booking agent had thoroughly checked him out before renting out his house—although it had turned out that the booking agent was a friend of his! But she certainly should have tried to find out some hard facts about him before blithely agreeing to be his house guest.

A minute later she heard the car start up, so she knew Zack had left the house. That meant she couldn't go and find him, plant herself in front of him and demand answers to all the questions that were running through her head. By early evening he still hadn't returned, so Nell cooked herself an evening meal and then limped slowly up to her room.

She sat by the window and watched the sun finally set behind the hills in a blaze of shimmering golden light that slowly dulled to a soft glow and then faded into darkness. Night had completely fallen by the time she heard the car return, the front door of the farmhouse open, then close again. Nell nervously nibbled her bottom lip and decided her questions would have to wait until morning. She didn't want to confront him at night.

For some reason, the combination of Zack and the warm velvet darkness outside unsettled her. She was sure she would feel a lot more confident in bright daylight.

She had expected to lie awake half the night, brooding over everything that had happened. Instead, though, she fell asleep surprisingly quickly, and didn't wake up again until early next morning.

Her bruises seemed a little less stiff after her undisturbed sleep, and when she put her foot to the ground she was relieved to find that her ankle had improved as well.

Nell went over to the window and looked out. The sun was only just beginning to rise, and the valley below and the hills beyond were still in soft shadow. The air was already warm, though, birds were trilling away happily, and it should have been the start of another splendid day. None of her days had been very splendid lately, though, and she wasn't at all certain they were going to improve in the future.

And this morning she had to go down and try to get some answers from Zack to at least some of her questions. Zack Hilliard, Nell repeated—it suited him better than 'Jackson Paine'. She said his name again a couple of times, but then abruptly stopped when she realised she was beginning to like the sound of it.

She had a long, leisurely bath, washed her hair, then sat by the window and let the long, dark strands dry in the sunshine. She was in no hurry to rush downstairs, for this latest confrontation. Finally, though, she pulled on jeans and a T-shirt, and went down to the kitchen.

Zack had obviously got up before her. There was warm coffee in the pot, and signs that he had already eaten breakfast. He wasn't in the kitchen, though, and she couldn't hear him moving around the house.

A quick glance out of the window confirmed that the car was still there. So where was he? wondered Nell. She made fresh coffee and drank it, then began to tap her fingers together thoughtfully. Perhaps he had gone for a walk—which meant she had the house to herself.

This might be a good time to try and find out a little more about Zack Hilliard, she decided, her pulses quickening slightly. How to do it, though? And what did she want to find out, first of all?

His real name, she told herself firmly. That would be a starting point for all the other things she needed to know about him. But to discover his name, she would have to find personal papers and letters, or maybe his passport. She gave a small, nervous gulp as she realised it would mean going through his possessions. She would have to search his room.

She wouldn't have to do it if he would only volunteer more information about himself, she argued with herself, trying to excuse what she was about to do. And she *did* have the right to know more about him. After all, her personal safety could be at stake.

Before she went anywhere near anything that belonged to him, though, she wanted to make *very* sure he wasn't in the farmhouse. She slowly made her way through all the rooms, occasionally calling his name. There wasn't any reply, and a long, careful look outside confirmed that he wasn't on the terrace or in the garden.

If she was going to do it, then it had to be now, Nell told herself. She might not get another chance. As quickly as she could, she made her way upstairs, her pulses positively racing.

Zack's room was at the far end of the farmhouse. With her heart thundering away in tune with her galloping pulses, she got as far as the door. Then she found she couldn't open it. Her conscience simply wouldn't let her. No matter what the circumstances, it was wrong to ransack through someone's private possessions without their permission.

Nell gave a deep sigh and turned away. What was she going to do now?

A door at the far end of the landing caught her attention, and she realised it led to a room she hadn't seen yet. Slowly she walked towards it. Surely it wouldn't hurt just to look inside? She wouldn't touch anything, only take a quick look, to see if it would yield any clues.

She opened the door and peeped round it. Then her eyes widened with surprise.

She was looking at a fairly large, airy room, which had been converted into a study. Shelves full of books lined the walls, there were a couple of filing cabinets, and a large desk by the window, on which sat a word processor. The desk was covered with stacks of paper, in a kind of ordered chaos, and folders were piled up on a chair beside the desk.

Nell stepped further inside and looked round with growing curiosity. She hadn't expected to find anything like this! She didn't touch the papers on the desk, but she did peer at the shelves that lined the walls. There were a lot of reference books, as if someone did a lot of research in this room, and a varied selection of fiction and non-fiction. Then Nell blinked because, tucked away on one of the top shelves in the corner, was a row of novels—by Jackson Paine!

When she had first seen the name in the newspaper, she had thought it sounded faintly familiar. Now she realised where she had heard it before. Jackson Paine wrote thrillers—very *good* thrillers. A couple had even been made into films. If she hadn't been so wrapped in her own problems and confused by her increasingly topsy-turvy emotions, she would have recognised the name sooner.

With a slightly unsteady hand, she took down one of the books. Inside the dust jacket at the back was a photograph of the author—a photograph of Zack!

'Zack is Jackson Paine?' she said out loud to herself, in bewilderment.

She put the book back and took down another one, as if she really needed to convince herself. There was the same photo inside the dust jacket, though, Zack with his shaggy dark hair, and his strong, sensual mouth. And his vivid blue eyes seemed to be looking at her slightly mockingly, as if he could actually see her confusion.

Then a hand seemed to appear from nowhere and whipped the book right out of her fingers. Nell jumped violently. Then, very, very slowly, she turned round. She already knew who that hand belonged to, and she wasn't in any hurry to see Zack's face. She had the feeling she wasn't going to like what she saw there.

Even when she was finally facing him, she kept her eyes downcast. Zack slid his fingers under her chin, though, and hooked her face up so that she had to meet his blazing blue eyes.

'Do you enjoy prying?' he demanded tersely.

'I'm not prying,' she muttered.

'Then what are you doing in here?' he asked, with clear contempt in his voice.

'I wanted to find out more about you,' Nell said defensively. 'I wanted to know who you really are.'

'What makes you think you've got the right to invade my privacy?'

'The fact that you won't tell me anything about yourself,' she retorted, with far more courage than she actually felt. 'First you tell me you're Zack Hilliard, then that newspaper gave your name as Jackson Paine. I didn't feel safe being here with a man who wouldn't even tell me his real name.'

'I did tell you my real name. I'm Zack Hilliard.'

'But you're also Jackson Paine!'

He shrugged. 'I didn't see any reason why you should know that.'

'You're a man with a lot of secrets,' Nell said accusingly.

'No, I'm not. I simply like my privacy.'

She began to recover a little from the shock of finding out the connection between Zack and Jackson Paine.

'Is that why you write under a pseudonym?' she asked.

'It makes life a lot easier, makes travel less of a hassle, if my real name isn't familiar to people. Writers are rarely recognised by their faces, they're usually only recognised by their names. If I signed into a hotel as Jackson Paine, by the end of the first evening I'd be surrounded by people offering ideas for stories, or wanting me to look at something they've written. If I sign in under my real name, just very occasionally someone recognises my face from a dust jacket, but usually no one bothers me.'

Nell blinked. She was still finding it very hard to take all this in. She had even read a couple of his books—and enjoyed them. Although she wasn't ready to admit that, at the moment!

'Are you working on a book right now?' she said at last.

'I'm still gathering material. I'll be ready to start on the book itself by the end of the month.'

'Why was there that article about you in the newspaper?'

'I've just signed a new contract with a big American publisher,' Zack replied, after a short pause. 'And a film deal for my next couple of books goes along with the contract. For some reason, the papers think that's newsworthy.'

'The article said "*un milione*",' Nell said slowly. 'That means a million, doesn't it? But a million of what? Lira?'

Zack's eyes narrowed a fraction. 'No,' he said curtly. 'Dollars. And the publishers think that's a fairly conservative estimate.'

'Contracts like that usually mean a lot of publicity and hype, to sell the books and promote the films,' she said slowly. 'You won't be able to go on living like a recluse, here in Tuscany.'

'I don't live like a recluse all the time. I've also got a flat in London. And a social life. I only come here when I need to get down to some hard work, without any distractions.'

Nell thought it highly likely that those distractions included the women that featured in his social life. And she was sure he had a very *full* social life! She had begun to realise that Zack wasn't just highly desirable and eligible, he was *rich*, highly desirable and eligible. For a certain kind of woman—usually young, beautiful, and on the lookout for financial security—that was an irresistible combination.

A mental picture of Zack being chased by a group of gorgeous blondes flitted through her mind. She should have laughed at it—but instead she was highly alarmed to feel a sharp twinge of jealousy.

Afraid he might see it, she quickly tried to cover it up. 'Well, at least I don't need to feel nervous about staying here any more,' she said, in an over-bright voice. 'I know exactly who you are now.'

A strange smile touched the corners of Zack's mouth. 'I thought it might make a difference.'

Something in his tone made her look up at him sharply. 'What do you mean?'

'You're a girl who likes celebrities, aren't you? And now you've found out that, in my own way, *I'm* one. I always knew that would make a difference to the way you felt about me,' he said in a cynical tone.

'Do you think——?' she began hotly.

'Oh, yes, I do think,' cut in Zack. 'My guess is that your attitude towards me is about to change.'

'It certainly is not!' Nell denied furiously.

His mouth curled into a smile that was as cynical as his tone, and he didn't even bother to reply.

Nell wasn't going to leave it at that, though. 'What do you think I'm going to do?' she demanded. 'Suddenly start chasing after you, just because I've found out that you're rich and famous? And about to become a lot richer?'

Zack shrugged. 'It's what girls like you do, isn't it?'

'Girls like me?' she repeated, in an outraged voice. 'You don't even *know* me, you've got no idea what I'm like!'

'Oh, but I do,' he said, his tone suddenly becoming hard. 'Those big brown eyes, that beautiful silken dark hair, the kind of face and body that can haunt a man's dreams for the rest of his life—I've seen them all before.'

'You can't have! We've never met before!'

'But I've met someone just like you,' Zack said, his eyes like blue ice now, as they fixed on her face. 'A girl who likes men with money, fame and influence, men who can buy her a career and guarantee all the publicity she craves.'

Nell had almost stopped breathing, because she had realised he was no longer talking about her. 'Who—who was she?' she asked in a cracked tone. 'Who did you know like that?'

'After my mother died, she was the girl my father married,' Zack said harshly.

'Your—your father?'

'Alec Hilliard. Heard of him?' he challenged her.

Nell realised she had. Alec Hilliard had been a top industrialist, owning and running one of the biggest conglomerates in the country. He had married a girl fifteen years younger than he was, a singer who was absolutely determined to get to the top. Alec Hilliard had poured vast amounts of money into promoting her career, had paid for records to be produced with top musicians and sound recordists, had subsidised concert tours, and used his influential contacts to provide her with endless publicity. The whole wildly extravagant venture had failed, though, because his young wife simply hadn't had the talent to make it as a top-rate singer.

Inevitably, the marriage had then deteriorated into divorce. And what a divorce it had been! Nell could clearly remember the endless newspaper coverage, as Alec Hilliard's wife made wilder and wilder accusations against her husband, demanded vast sums of money in settlement, and revelled in the accompanying publicity which she adored and craved.

Three months after the divorce had become final, Alec Hilliard had died. The official verdict was a heart attack, but many people thought his heart hadn't failed, but had simply been broken.

Nell swallowed very hard. 'It—it must have been a hard time for you.'

'Hard?' echoed Zack, a little incredulously. 'It was sheer hell! But at least it taught me all about beautiful, ambitious girls who'll do absolutely anything for publicity, anything to further their own careers.'

'And you think that's the kind of girl *I* am?' she said in a choked voice.

'Until you convince me otherwise, I think it's a lot safer to go on assuming that's exactly the kind of girl you are,' Zack said grimly.

They stared at each other, and Nell was the first one to look away.

I don't care what this man thinks of me, she told herself fiercely. It doesn't matter, it isn't important. But she was very much afraid that was beginning to be a lie.

Quite suddenly she wanted to get out of this room. She hated being pinned down by that cynical blue gaze. Zack was blocking the doorway, though. She couldn't get past without pushing him out of the way—and she guessed he was a man who never let himself be pushed by anyone.

She licked her lips, then realised that her entire mouth had gone uncomfortably dry. Perhaps it was because Zack was now looking directly at her, his eyes narrowing into an unnervingly intense gaze.

He moved nearer, and then still nearer, and she immediately wanted to scurry away, to run and keep on running, but that was impossible. For one thing, her ankle would simply give way. And for another, she had been slowly retreating as he had moved towards her, and she could feel the wall now pressing against her back. He had forced her into the corner—she couldn't get away from him. What was he up to? she wondered with a small inner shiver.

His eyes were alight now with a mixture of desire and contempt. No man had ever looked at her in that way before, and Nell shivered all over again.

'Don't—don't come any closer,' she warned shakily.

'I shouldn't want to come near you at all,' he said softly. 'There are so many things about you that I don't like, that I despise. They ought to be enough to keep me away from you—but it doesn't work like that, does it, Nell?'

The way he said her name sent a whole new set of shivers running through her.

'I really want you to go away,' she said doggedly.

Zack didn't move an inch. 'I don't think you want me to go away at all.'

'I certainly do!' she lied. 'You shouldn't be doing this, you're deliberately intimidating me, making me feel—feel——'

'Frightened?' he suggested.

'Yes,' muttered Nell.

'You're not frightened of me. You never have been.'

'I certainly am,' she insisted. 'You're over six foot, and I hardly come up to your shoulder. And you won't let me out of this room. *That's* frightening.'

'You can walk past me. I won't try to stop you.'

But Nell's legs wouldn't seem to work. She just stood there and trembled, pinned down by something that she didn't even understand. Her heart was hammering away with almost painful hardness, and something very odd seemed to have happened to her breathing.

'I want you to go away,' she repeated again in a strangled voice.

'I don't think you do,' Zack said again.

He lifted his hand and let it move slowly towards her. Nell watched it, half hypnotised by its gentle progress, her breathing almost grinding to a halt.

'Don't touch me,' she managed to whisper when his long, well-shaped fingers were barely an inch away from the soft curve of her breast.

'Why not?' he said softly. 'Because we don't like each other? But this has nothing to do with liking. On the other hand,' he went on, his mouth relaxing into a more sensual line, 'perhaps we shouldn't do this. We don't really know each other well enough yet for such intimacies, do we?'

His hand stayed exactly where it was, though; she only had to breathe a little harder and the tight, aching tip of her breast would brush against his waiting fingertips.

Nell held her breath. She wouldn't move, she vowed. Not until he backed away from her.

A slow smile began to touch his lips, as if he knew exactly what she was doing, and was enjoying her confusion.

'You can't hold your breath for ever,' he told her at last. 'What do you suppose is going to happen when you breathe out, Nell?'

'Please take your hand away,' she said in a choked voice.

'I'm not sure I want to.' There was a soft purr in his voice now.

Nell tried to say something, but she didn't have enough breath left. Her lungs felt as if they were going to burst, she was getting dizzy from lack of oxygen, and she finally couldn't stop herself from breathing out with a loud gasp. Her body sagged forward at the same time, but as she braced herself against Zack's touch he smoothly moved his hand away.

'You're playing games with me,' she accused, panting slightly.

'Men and women always play games with each other. Haven't you learnt that yet?'

'I don't like this kind of game!'

'I rather think you do. And if I'm right, then you won't mind that it isn't over yet.'

Before she could demand to know what he meant by that, he leant forward and his mouth swiftly covered hers.

She struggled against the kiss that followed, but couldn't escape from its hard intensity. The sheer power of it overwhelmed her. No kiss she had ever had before had been anything like it.

She was breathless all over again, but for an entirely different reason. Small shivers began to run right through her, right down to the very tips of her toes, and alarming sensations shot through all her nerve-ends.

Every instinct she had was warning her against this kiss, this man. What could she do about it, though? He wouldn't release her, and she couldn't escape—didn't want to escape. Nell just stood there and trembled as his mouth ravaged hers, plundering almost at leisure now as the shock of it reduced her to a quivering helplessness.

When Zack finally released her, his eyes were very bright and his own breathing wasn't entirely steady.

'Remember what I told you,' he said in a soft voice. 'You don't have to like someone to want to do something like that. And we don't like each other, do we, Nell?'

'No,' she lied, through bruised lips.

His vivid blue gaze swept over her, and a faintly mocking smile touched the corners of his mouth. 'Of course not. Now, I think you'd better get out of this room before we discover what else two people who dislike each other still want to do together.'

Nell didn't need to be told twice. She turned round and fled, slamming the door behind her as if she badly needed to put a physical barrier between herself and Zack Hilliard.

Of all the alarming and disturbing things that had happened to her recently, this came at the very top of the list!

CHAPTER SIX

To HER utter relief, Nell heard Zack leave the farm-house soon after that. He took the car and drove off at some speed. Nell hoped it would be a while before he came back again. She definitely needed some time on her own, to think over all the things she had learnt about him today. And everything that had happened between them.

She licked her bruised lips and found she could still taste his kiss. That bothered her. In fact, every single thing that had happened over the last couple of days bothered her. And she was definitely shaken by her nerve-jarring reaction to that kiss. A lot more than just body chemistry caused that!

At least she understood a lot more things, now, though. She certainly knew why Zack had looked at her with such contempt when he had first found out who she was. Nell gave a slightly despairing shake of her head. How he must hate the kind of girl he thought her to be; the kind who deliberately courted publicity of any kind, good or bad. She could only guess at the hell he must have been through as he had seen his father destroyed by a turbulent marriage to such a girl.

To her alarm, Nell found she desperately wanted to convince him she wasn't like that, that she had been the victim of a highly efficient publicity machine. Two things stopped her, though. The first was the un-comfortable thought that, at the beginning, she had willingly gone along with everything that had hap-pened between her and Lloyd Kendrick. For a while, she had enjoyed being the centre of attention, had got a kick out of seeing her photo in the papers. She was also rather ashamed to admit that it had been mar-vellous for her ego, being chased after and courted by the sexy, famous Lloyd Kendrick. That surely made her partly responsible for everything else that had happened to her? she thought miserably.

And the second thing that stopped her was the knowledge that, while Zack had such a low opinion of her, she was a lot safer.

She had already been highly disturbed by the way she reacted to him. And just before he had kissed her, she had seen the hot gleam that had briefly lit his own eyes. But if he went on thoroughly despising her, surely he would stop himself from taking things any further? she argued with herself. Zack was a man with a grim determination not to let history repeat itself. To keep him at bay, all she had to do was to reinforce his already low opinion of her.

And I *do* want to keep him at bay, she told herself with some determination.

Zack didn't return to the farmhouse for several hours. In fact, darkness had fallen by the time she heard the car finally pulling up outside. She was up-stairs in her room, drying her hair after a shower. She began to move towards the door, ready to go down to meet him, then she stopped herself. Perhaps it would be better to stay where she was. Why risk another confrontation, when it wasn't necessary? Anyway, she wasn't sure she wanted to look into those vivid blue eyes again so soon. Sometimes she thought they could see right inside her head—even inside her soul. Nell gave a small, involuntary shiver, because there was the awful temptation to feel fascinated by the thought of someone being able to do that.

Still fully dressed, she flopped down on the bed. Quite suddenly she felt very tired. Over these last few weeks she had discovered that emotional wear and tear could be far more exhausting than strenuous physical exercise.

Her heavy eyes slid shut, and just seconds later she fell straight into a deep sleep. After a while she began to dream, and they were the kind of dreams that made her move around restlessly and mutter incoherently under her breath. She didn't wake up, though, and after a while she became still again and slept through more peacefully until morning.

When she woke up, she found she felt slightly better, a little more in control. Not a *lot* better, she told herself with a wry grimace. She had the feeling it was going to be a long time before she began to feel really good again about her life. She felt more able to cope with things this morning, though. Even the memory of that kiss was fading. At least, that was what she told herself—several times—until she was almost convinced.

After a shower, she quickly dressed and went downstairs. Her ankle had improved to the point where she was only limping on it slightly, and the bruises were fading to an unsightly yellow. Another couple of days and they would be hardly noticeable.

Nell pushed open the door to the kitchen, and felt her stomach muscles involuntarily tighten when she saw that Zack was already there. It seemed to be an automatic reaction now, whenever she saw him. Apart from that, though, she was pleased to find that her nerves felt surprisingly steady. That long sleep had obviously done her good.

'Want some coffee?' he offered, as she came in.

'Yes, please,' she said, sitting down at the far side of the table so that there was a safe distance between them.

Zack poured the coffee, then let his blue gaze come up to rest on her slightly flushed face.

'Are you still angry about yesterday?' he asked calmly.

'I certainly didn't like what you did,' she forced herself to say at once.

'I think we've already been over what we like—and don't like,' he reminded her, making her flush even deeper. 'The only question left is, do you still want to stay on here?'

'I don't have anywhere else to go, except back to England. And you know very well I don't want to go there.'

'Still pretending you're trying to avoid publicity?'

'I *am* trying to avoid it,' Nell said hotly.

Zack merely shrugged. 'So you say. Either way, it really isn't any concern of mine. I simply want to know if you're staying or not.'

'Yes, I'm going to stay,' Nell found herself saying, without quite realising when she had made that decision. 'As long as you don't jump on me again,' she added pointedly.

His mouth relaxed into an unexpected and wolfish smile. 'I never jump on women. I prefer lovemaking to be very slow and sensual. Each small peak of pleasure stretched to its limits. Every touch drawn out until you ache for the next one.'

The low purr of his voice did extraordinary things to her nervous system. It practically sat up and begged for more!

She gave an audible gulp and hastily pulled herself together.

'There wasn't anything very slow about that kiss yesterday,' she made herself retort. '*Or* gentle.' Then she was immediately angry with herself. She hadn't meant to mention that kiss at all!

Zack was already looking at her consideringly, though. 'That kiss was something of an experiment,' he said at last. 'A way of finding out a couple of things I needed to know.'

'What kind of things?' she asked warily.

He didn't answer, though. For some reason, that made her even more edgy.

'I just want to know that you're not going to kiss me again like that,' she said rather defiantly.

'Oh, no, I won't kiss you again quite like that,' he said softly.

His voice had become almost velvety, and Nell was dismayed by the way her pulses instantly leapt in response. Get hold of yourself, she instructed herself fiercely. He's doing this to you on purpose. He's trying to throw you off balance. Anyway, what had he meant by that ambiguous answer? That he wouldn't kiss her again, or that the next kiss would be very different? She didn't know—and didn't dare ask!

In fact, she decided it was time she brought this entire conversation to a close. She got to her feet and picked up her rapidly cooling cup of coffee.

'I'm going out on to the terrace,' she told him.

As she hurried out of the kitchen, though, Zack stood up and followed her. Nerves jangling, Nell swung round to face him.

'Will you please stop following me?' she snapped.

'I'm not following you, I simply wanted to issue an invitation,' Zack said in a more relaxed tone of voice.

'Invitation?' she echoed suspiciously. 'What kind of invitation?'

'I've got a business meeting in Florence today. I thought you might like to come with me. We could go a couple of hours early, if you like, and I'll show you some of the sights.'

'Why do you want me to come with you?' she asked, still suspicious.

'No ulterior motive. You've hardly left the house since you arrived, and although the views are fairly impressive you must be getting rather tired of them by now. I thought you'd like a change of scene.'

'What about your business meeting? Won't I be in the way?'

'Sam's a friend, as well as a business partner. We're meeting over lunch, it's going to be a very relaxed affair, and there won't be any problem if you join us.'

Nell thought it over. Would it be a good idea to go to Florence with him? To spend more time with him, so soon after everything that had happened yesterday?

On the other hand, she was longing to get out of the house for a few hours. And there wouldn't be any problems in a crowded city like Florence. With all those people around, what could possibly happen? Come to think of it, she would be far safer there than she was here in this isolated farmhouse. And they would be joined by Sam, Zack's business colleague. That would make it doubly safe.

Then she remembered something else, and her face fell.

'I can't go to Florence,' she said dolefully. 'What if someone recognises me? My picture's been in the papers so often recently, I sometimes think everyone in the world must know my face!'

'Would a little more publicity really worry you?' asked Zack, a definite chill returning to his tone.

'Yes, believe it or not! And you've made it very clear that it would certainly worry *you*,' she retorted. 'And remember, I'll be with you. That'll make us both the centre of attention.'

'Then put on a pair of dark glasses and tie back your hair,' he advised. 'That should be enough to make you look fairly anonymous. Anyway, I don't think it'll be a problem. Florence is going to be full of tourists, not journalists. And people on holiday are generally only interested in having a good time; they're too busy seeing the sights and enjoying themselves to notice if someone's face looks vaguely familiar.' Then he glanced at his watch. 'If you want to see some of the sights before lunch, we'd better leave right now. I'll give you ten minutes to get ready. And wear something cool—it'll be hot and crowded in the city centre.'

Nell hurried upstairs, and when she came down again—nine and a half minutes later—she had changed into a thin cotton skirt, with a sleeveless matching top. She had twisted her hair into a long plait and not bothered to put on any make-up, and a glance in the mirror had told her it made her look about sixteen. That had made her smile a little grimly, because over the last couple of weeks she had often felt three times that age!

She felt Zack look at her in surprise as she came down.

'Anonymous enough?' she asked wryly.

'You look like a schoolgirl. A very tempting schoolgirl,' he added with an odd twist of his mouth.

A little flustered, Nell fished a large pair of sunglasses out of her bag and put them on. Zack immediately walked over and took them off again, though.

'I need them,' she protested with a small frown. 'They hide half my face.'

'You can put them on again when we reach Florence. In the meantime, I want to be able to see your eyes.'

'Why?' she asked guardedly.

'Because they give away more than you ever do,' he told her, to her consternation.

While she digested that thoroughly uncomfortable piece of information, Zack walked out to the car, leaving her to trail along behind him with her dark brows slightly drawn together.

He started up the car, and they headed down the track that led away from the farmhouse. The sun shone down out of the clear blue sky, the hills all around them basked gently in its heat, and they left faint clouds of dust behind them as Zack drove expertly along the narrow roads. They zipped past a vineyard, with its rows of vines that striped the hillside, and then the road began to climb again and a small hill town came into sight, basking tranquilly in the hot sunshine. A tall bell tower loomed over the jumble of roofs that were etched against the deep blue of the sky, and the honey-coloured walls glowed in the golden light of the sun.

'You've never been to Florence before?' asked Zack a couple of minutes later.

'No, I haven't.'

'Why not? Isn't it one of the places that everyone wants to visit if they possibly can?'

'There's never been much money to spare for trips abroad,' she said ruefully. 'Unless you're at the very top, you don't make much money out of acting. Most of the time you're resting, and fitting in all sorts of part-time jobs just to make ends meet.'

'Sell your story to the papers, and you'll have all the money you'll need for the next year or so,' he pointed out rather more coolly.

Nell was about to say very angrily that she would never, *ever* do that, when she remembered that this might be a good time to try and reinforce his low opinion of her. She had already decided she would be much safer if he thought she really was ambitious for money and fame. He certainly wouldn't want to get involved with that kind of girl, after what had happened to his father.

'How much do you suppose I'd get?' she made herself ask.

Zack gave a dark scowl, as if he didn't like her answer.

'I've no idea,' he said curtly. 'But I suppose they pay well for that kind of trash. Just make sure you leave my house before you get in touch with them, though. If I pick up the phone and there's a journalist on the other end, or I find one camping on my doorstep——'

He didn't finish the sentence—but he didn't need to. Just the tone of his voice made Nell suddenly feel very cold. She also felt a sudden need to change the conversation.

'Are you going to stay in Tuscany for the rest of the summer?' she asked.

'I'll probably go back to my flat in London for a couple of weeks at the end of the month,' he replied, after a short pause. 'I can't live like a monk for too long,' he added more wryly.

'And you have to, here in Italy?'

The grim line of his mouth finally relaxed into a faint smile. 'Italian girls are usually very closely chaperoned.'

'Then perhaps you ought to marry one,' Nell suggested. 'That would solve all your problems. How about the beautiful Maria, Signora Ginelli's daughter? *Is* she beautiful?' she asked a little wistfully.

'Yes, she is,' Zack said without hesitation.

Nell fought back a definite pang of jealousy. 'Then wouldn't she make the perfect wife?'

'She probably would,' he agreed. More jealousy surged relentlessly through Nell's veins before he added, 'But not for me.'

She was just feeling a little happier when another thought occurred to her. 'There's—there's someone back in London?'

'There are several "someones" back in London,' he said drily. 'And all of them are usually very pleased to see me.'

'Are you eventually going to marry one of them?'

He gave a small growl of exasperation. 'Why this sudden desire to marry me off? At the moment, I've no intention of marrying anyone at all. And if I ever do, then I'll pick my wife very carefully indeed. I've seen the sheer hell that can result if you get it wrong.'

Nell bit her lip, because she knew he was thinking about his father. 'What——?' she began hesitantly. Then she got a little more of her nerve back. 'What if you fall in love with someone quite unsuitable?'

'That won't happen,' he said at once.

'It happens to lots of people all the time,' she argued.

'Not to me,' he said flatly. 'I won't let it.'

And she believed him.

'Of course, I wouldn't rule out a purely sexual relationship with such a person,' Zack went on.

Nell's nerves gave a severe jolt. 'You—you wouldn't?' she queried in a suddenly squeaky voice.

He shrugged. 'It's one way of getting it out of your system. Frustrated love can lead to obsession, and obsession is dangerous. Much better to let it burn itself out in bed.'

'I—I don't think you could do that,' she said a little unsteadily.

'Of course I could,' he said, and there was a dark glint in his eyes now. 'Take you, for example, Nell.'

'M-me?' she stammered.

'There's something about you that turns me on. But you know that, don't you? I don't like it, because your lifestyle turns my stomach, but I can't pretend it isn't happening. If you agreed, I'd probably go to bed with you. But it would never go any further than that.'

'Well, I certainly *wouldn't* agree,' she said vehemently.

'I didn't think you would. I'm simply saying I know the difference between love and sex. And I also know how to keep the two well apart.'

Nell's heart was thumping so hard it was making her head spin. Zack was telling her he wanted her, but he would never let her be anything more than physically close to him. This was even more dangerous than she had thought!

You've got to make him stop even wanting you, she told herself with a touch of panic. Because it would be all too easy to want him back—and that would be a recipe for absolute disaster!

Zack didn't say anything more, but he didn't need to. Nell's nervous system had already been thrown into complete disarray. For the first time she seriously contemplated leaving the farmhouse before her two weeks were up. All right, so she would have to go back and face the Press—which she absolutely dreaded—but staying on could have even more catastrophic consequences. When they returned from Florence, perhaps she would ring a travel agent, see what arrangements would have to be made.

In the meantime, she definitely had to keep Zack at arm's length. How to do it, though? How to make sure he gave up all thoughts of wanting her in any way at all?

After a lot of frantic thinking, a glimmer of an idea began to form inside her head. His opinion of her was already very low. Perhaps she could make it sink still further, until it finally reached rock bottom. And if, on top of that, she really began to grate on his nerves, if she irritated and exasperated him beyond bearing, that would surely make him forget all thoughts of wanting to take her to bed? No one could go on wanting someone who really got on their nerves.

The more she thought about it, the more the idea appealed to her. She was sure she could make it work—after all, she was an actress, wasn't she? And she would start right now. That revealing conversation with Zack had made it a fairly urgent priority!

Although Florence was packed with cars, Zack soon found a place to park.

'We'll have to walk to the centre of the city from here,' he told her. 'It's a pedestrian area, so we can't take the car any further. It isn't far, though, we can easily walk it in a few minutes. And there'll be plenty of time for you to see some of the best parts of Florence before lunch.'

'But it's rather hot to keep walking around,' said Nell, making her tone sound deliberately plaintive. 'And my ankle still hurts.'

'When you walked out to the car this morning, you weren't even limping on it.'

She gave a brave little smile. 'I was hiding the pain. I don't like to complain.'

Zack shot a suspicious look at her. 'Why didn't you mention it before we set out?'

'I didn't want you to worry about me,' she said, trying to sound noble. 'But now that we're here, I suppose I ought to try and see some of the sights. If you'll be patient with me, I'll do the very best I can.'

She got out of the car and set off very slowly down the street, hobbling noticeably. Zack locked the car and strode after her, quickly catching up with her. Then he had to slow his pace down to a crawl, as Nell continued to make her way down the street at a snail's pace. She could see him fighting to contain his impatience, and stifled a grin. This was a good start. She would make sure that, by the end of the day, Zack was so thoroughly sick and tired of her that he would do everything he could to avoid her. He would certainly have forgotten any thoughts he might have once had about wanting to take her to bed!

The streets were narrow, crowded and hot. Nell would soon have got lost, but Zack obviously knew exactly where he was going.

They eventually came out into a square dominated by the great cathedral, Santa Maria del Fiore, with its magnificent dome that featured on almost every postcard view of Florence. It was faced with coloured marble, and with the equally ornate bell tower beside it Nell had to admit it was an impressive and beautiful sight. At least, she was willing to admit it to herself. There was no way she was going to say it to Zack!

Opposite stood the Baptistry, one of the oldest buildings in Florence.

'The doors of the Baptistry were designed by Lorenzo Ghiberti, and it took him twenty-seven years to create them,' Zack told her.

'Really?' said Nell, giving a small but obvious yawn.

His face darkened a fraction. 'Don't you even want to look at them?'

'One door's very much like another, isn't it?' she said, managing to sound polite but bored.

'Hardly,' Zack growled. 'Even Michelangelo described them as being "worthy of gracing the entrance to Paradise".'

Nell was actually dying to see the world-famous doors, but she somehow managed to shrug and look uninterested. Zack's face grew even darker, but he held on to his temper.

'Fine,' he said shortly, 'if you don't want to see the doors, we'll move on.'

They left the square, making their way along more narrow streets thronged with tourists. Nell walked even slower this time, and Zack's long stride kept carrying him ahead of her.

'Please don't walk so fast,' she said politely, as he stopped yet again to allow her to catch up.

He muttered something under his breath, and when she was sure he was looking the other way, she gave a small grin. This was fun! And as long as she was careful and didn't let him see she was doing it on purpose, she was perfectly safe.

The street led them into the Piazza della Signoria, with the Palazzo Vecchio rising majestically at the far end, its tall, crenellated bell tower silhouetted impressively against the blue of the sky. Nell looked at it with a rather blank expression, determined not to let Zack know that she adored it here in the centre of Florence; that she would have given her right arm for the chance to explore properly, and see all the wonderful treasures and beautiful buildings that were gathered here.

Instead, she walked slowly over to the Fountain of Neptune and looked briefly at the great statue that dominated it. Then she glanced at the other statues in front of the Palazzo, finally stopping in front of the copy of Michelangelo's David.

Zack stood beside her as she gazed up at it for a few seconds.

'Very nice,' she said at last, in a totally unimpressed voice.

'Nice?' Zack exploded. 'You're looking at a copy of probably the most famous statue in the world! Can't you find another word to describe it except "nice"?'

'I did say it was *very* nice,' Nell said in a rather hurt voice.

He looked at her with some disbelief. Then he shook his head. 'Let's move on. We'll cross the river by the

Ponte Vecchio—although you'll probably think that's just a "very nice bridge",' he added with some sarcasm.

Nell found it hard to stop her eyes darting around, drinking in all the details, as they made their way across the Ponte Vecchio. When Zack stopped in the centre to look at the familiar view down the River Arno, with the hills that surrounded Florence shimmering gently in the distance, in the heat, she had to force herself to keep on moving. She didn't even allow herself to glance at the goldsmiths' and silversmiths' shops that lined the bridge.

When they reached the other side, Zack began to walk along the side of the river. Nell deliberately trailed behind. He glanced round a couple of times, his face darkening again, and she felt a glow of satisfaction. This was really working remarkably well! Why hadn't she thought of this tactic before? Men could stand a lot of things, but they would always be completely turned off by a woman who really grated on their nerves.

'Where are we going now?' she called after him, and this time she managed to put a rather aggravating whine into her voice.

Zack swung back to face her, and his blue eyes registered clear impatience. 'There's a view I want you to see. If you're not impressed with it, then I'll give up. We'll go and meet Sam for lunch, and forget about seeing the sights of Florence.'

'Is it far?' she asked with a wan sigh.

'Not far, but you will have to go up a couple of steep paths.'

Nell decided that it was time to start hobbling again. 'I'll do the best I can,' she said, in the kind of martyred voice that was guaranteed to drive any man to distraction.

Zack was no exception. 'The exercise will do you good,' he growled. Then, without even looking at her, he turned round and strode off.

The paths that he led her up were steep, and her ankle was giving a couple of genuine twinges by the time they reached the top. When she finally stepped into the large square at the top, though, Nell knew she would have hopped up here, if necessary, in order not to miss this view.

The whole of Florence was spread out below them, a sea of pale walls and jumbled, red-tiled roofs. Church spires and bell towers soared into the air, the great dome of the cathedral almost seemed to float above the city, and the River Arno wound its way into the distance, crossed by a string of bridges, with the Ponte Vecchio taking pride of place. And beyond the panoramic view of the city lay the hills that surrounded Florence, gently undulating into the distance, taking on a dreamy blue haze in the heat of midday.

Nell could have gazed at the view for hours. Just in time, though, she remembered that she shouldn't be looking wide-eyed and impressed. Hurriedly she arranged her face into a faintly bored expression.

'Yes, it's a very pleasant view,' she said politely. Then, in a more plaintive voice, she went on, 'Is it time for lunch yet? I'm starving!'

'Don't you have any soul, woman?' Zack almost roared at her. 'You've got all Florence spread out at your feet, and all you can think about is food?'

'Well, I'm sorry,' she said, letting her bottom lip quiver slightly. 'I've already said it's a pleasant view. What more do you want me to say?'

'Nothing,' he growled at her. Then his blue eyes narrowed as they fixed on her. 'If I thought for one moment that you were doing this on purpose——' he said more slowly.

Nell's heart almost stopped beating. She swallowed hard, and made a huge effort to keep her voice steady. 'Doing what on purpose?' she asked, letting her own eyes grow wide and innocent. Then she gave a small yawn, as if she were beginning to find the conversation very boring. 'I really am hungry. When can we eat?'

'Right now,' Zack said shortly. He strode off, and Nell followed at a more sedate pace, feeling more and more pleased with herself.

This was working out even better than she had hoped. For the first time since Zack Hilliard had erupted into her life, she felt that she was in control of the situation. She intended to hold on to that feeling for as long as she could.

CHAPTER SEVEN

BACK in the centre of the city, Nell followed Zack as he led her towards one of the restaurants. His temper was obviously becoming increasingly short, but that didn't worry her. There were too many people around; he wouldn't risk causing a scene. A man who disliked publicity would definitely try to avoid drawing attention to himself in a public place. And Sam, his business colleague, would be joining them for lunch, so that would place further restraints on him.

Inside the restaurant, the décor was turn of the century, with stained glass and dark wood panelling. When Nell picked up the menu, she gave a small grin of satisfaction. Everything on it was disgustingly expensive! This would be another chance to convince Zack that she was a girl who was only interested in the good things of life.

Zack looked around with a brief frown. 'Sam isn't here yet,' he said shortly. 'Do you want a drink while we're waiting?'

Nell had a glass of wine, but by the time she had finished it there was still no sign of the elusive Sam.

'Your business colleague is very late,' she said to Zack.

'Punctuality has never been one of Sam's strong points.' He tapped his fingers a little impatiently.

'We'll have our lunch,' he decided. 'Perhaps Sam will turn up later.'

Nell chose a starter of toast spread with chicken-liver pâté, while Zack ran his gaze over the wine list which the waiter had just given him.

'Is there any particular wine you like?' he asked, handing the list over to her.

Instead of looking at the names of the wines, Nell simply looked at the prices listed beside them.

'That one,' she said without hesitation, pointing to the most expensive.

One of Zack's eyebrows gently twitched, but he didn't say a word. Instead, when the waiter returned, he quietly ordered the wine, then began to eat his own starter.

Nell had a delicious soup to follow, flavoured with rosemary, onions, celery and tomatoes, then chose *arista alla Fiorentina*, roast loin of pork which had been pierced and then the holes filled with rosemary and ground pepper. Zack had *bistecca alla Fiorentina*, which was a great wedge of steak seasoned with olive oil, salt and pepper. Sam still hadn't turned up, but Nell didn't particularly mind. She knew she would have felt rather out of place if he and Zack had wanted to discuss business.

The wine was very, very good—which was just as well, considering what it had cost! Nell told herself, as she finished a second glass. Zack didn't order any dessert, but she couldn't resist a big slice of sponge crammed with a filling of almonds, hazelnuts, chocolate and cream.

'Obviously you don't worry about your weight,' Zack said drily. 'For a small girl, you've put away a quite amazing amount of food.'

'I'm lucky,' she said, giving a small sigh of satisfaction as she finished the last of her dessert, 'I never put on any weight, no matter how much I eat. I think even I've had enough, though,' she added, with a small grin.

Zack signalled to the waiter for the bill. 'What other vices do you have, apart from gluttony?' he enquired, sitting back and looking at her.

'I'm not a glutton!' she denied indignantly. 'I simply enjoy food. And I don't have any other vices.' Then she remembered, rather belatedly, that she wanted him to have a very low opinion of her. 'Of course, I am ambitious,' she added hastily. 'I'd do anything to further my career. And I want to earn good money. Lots and *lots* of money. I don't think you can ever have too much of it, do you?'

Zack studied her, his blue eyes thoughtful. 'Money can certainly be very useful at times,' he agreed at last, almost too calmly.

There was something in his eyes that definitely disturbed her. She wasn't sure what it was, but she was absolutely positive it was there, a dark glint, a hidden warning of danger.

Nell felt a small shiver run right up her spine, and she was quite glad that the waiter came over at that point, bringing their bill and putting an end to that particular conversation.

Zack glanced at the bill. Then he took out his wallet, swiftly counted out some notes, and put them on the table.

Nell stared at the money suspiciously. 'That isn't enough to pay for our meal,' she said at last.

'It's enough to cover my half of the bill,' Zack told her coolly.

'Your half?' she yelped. Then she hurriedly lowered her voice as several nearby diners turned their heads and stared at her. 'What do you mean, your half?'

'You didn't expect me to pay for your lunch, did you?'

'Of course——' Her voice had begun to rise again. She made a small choked sound, and began again more quietly, but no less vehemently. 'Of course I did. You never said we were each going to pay for our own meal!'

His dark eyebrows rose delicately. 'I didn't think I needed to say it. We're not lovers, Nell. Or even friends. Why did you expect me to pay for you?'

'Because—well, because you invited me to lunch,' she said in an outraged voice. 'And you've just signed a contract for a million dollars. You can *afford* to pay.'

Zack gave a nonchalant shrug. 'I didn't invite you to lunch. If you remember, I said this was going to be a business lunch and you were welcome to join us. And as for that million dollars—I won't have it for very long if I fritter it away on greedy girls who like to eat and drink the most expensive items on the menu.'

Was that a gleam of laughter in his eyes? Nell thought furiously. Had he known from the very start what she was doing, and coolly decided he wasn't going to let her get away with it?

'I'm waiting for you to pay up your half of the bill,' he added.

'I can't do it,' she muttered. 'You'll——' She took a deep breath and shut her eyes because she hated having to say this. 'You'll have to lend it to me.'

'Isn't there one more word that you should have added there?' he asked pointedly.

Nell gritted her teeth. '*Please* will you lend me the money?'

'You realise that this will put you in my debt?' Zack said silkily.

'I'll pay back every single penny,' she muttered. Then she shot a rather panicky look at the maître d', who was hovering in the background, obviously aware that there had been a small hitch in the smooth running of his restaurant. This was the kind of place where they would make quite a fuss if someone tried to walk out without paying the bill!

To her utter relief, Zack produced his wallet again and took out enough notes to cover the cost of her meal. Then she began to wonder where she was going to find the extra money to pay him back. Perhaps she could persuade him to accept it in instalments? If only she hadn't eaten so much, she groaned silently. Or chosen that horrifyingly expensive bottle of wine!

Zack stood up. 'Time to leave,' he said. 'It's obvious that Sam isn't going to turn up.'

Nell was only too glad to get out of the restaurant. This latest part of her plan had gone badly wrong, and she was going to be paying for it—literally!—for a long time to come.

As they went back out into the crowded, sun-drenched street, Zack moved a little closer.

'I think you've learnt a valuable lesson today,' he murmured in her ear. 'Don't play games unless you're absolutely certain you can win.'

'I haven't been playing games,' she denied, hoping she would be forgiven for that whopping big lie.

'Of course you have,' he said calmly. 'But I don't think you'll do it again. And of course, you can forget about paying me back for that meal.'

'I intend to give you every single penny,' she insisted.

'I told you once before, I never take money from women.'

Nell abandoned the argument, because she felt utterly deflated. He knew exactly what she had been trying to do today—and had found a way of stopping her from getting away with it.

She suddenly decided she had had enough of Florence. She wanted to get away from the crowds, the heat, the rather overwhelming richness of the city.

'I think it's time we went back to the car,' she said in a low voice. She began to walk back along the narrow street, with Zack's easy stride easily keeping up with her.

'Your injured ankle seems to have improved amazingly since we left the restaurant,' he commented, a few moments later. 'This morning you could hardly hobble about. Now you look as if you could run a marathon!'

'You know very well there was very little wrong with my ankle,' she muttered.

'There are quite a lot of things I'm beginning to know about you,' Zack said thoughtfully. But before she could ask him exactly what he meant by that, someone suddenly called his name.

Nell looked round and saw a tall woman with beautiful cheekbones, a perfectly shaped mouth, sky-blue eyes and a mop of tumbled blonde curls.

'Zack!' said the woman again, coming towards them. 'Sorry I missed lunch, but a client turned up at the last moment, and I couldn't get away. I came rushing over as soon as he'd gone—I really wanted to see you.' Then she wound her arms around Zack's neck and kissed him full on the mouth, the kind of soft, intimate kiss that you only gave to a very close friend—or lover.

Nell found herself hit by a great bolt of pure jealousy. It zipped right through her, from head to toe, leaving her shaking a little because of its sheer intensity. She had never felt anything even remotely like it before, hadn't known she was capable of such white-hot emotion. She hardly even heard what Zack was saying.

'You always turn up late,' he said to the blonde woman, although without any rancour. 'By the way, this is Nell. She's my house guest at the moment. Nell, this is Sam—Samantha Harrington. She runs the agency through which you booked my farmhouse.'

'I run it, but Zack finances it,' said Sam, with a dazzling smile. 'He's a darling—without him I'd never have got it off the ground.'

Nell mumbled something rather incoherent. Neither of them seemed to notice, though. Sam was already talking again, one of her hands resting in a proprietorial way on Zack's arm.

'Look, I'm sorry about lunch, but I really need to talk to you. Perhaps we could discuss things over a cup of coffee?'

'That's fine with me,' said Zack easily. Then he turned to Nell. 'Do you want to join us?'

'No, thank you,' she said in a stiff voice. 'I'm sure you want to spend some time alone with your— friend.' She managed to put a wealth of meaning into that last word. 'If you give me the keys, I'll wait for you back at the car.'

'Are you sure you can find it?' asked Zack, handing over the keys.

'I'm not totally incompetent,' said Nell through gritted teeth. Then she quickly turned away and began to walk off, before either of them could notice that anything was wrong.

More by luck than any sense of direction, she found her way back to the car. It was very hot inside where the sun was burning right down on it, but Nell didn't even notice as she slumped on to the front seat. So, Sam was a woman. And Nell was quite sure she was a lot more than just a business partner! Her teeth clenched all over again as she remembered that kiss Sam had given Zack.

She tried to force herself to relax, aware that she was over-reacting. Then she began to wonder *why* she was over-reacting. After all, Zack was a free agent; he was entitled to have a whole string of friends—and lovers.

Unrestrained jealousy shot through her again as she pictured the beautiful Sam as Zack's lover. Then the jealousy was followed by a wave of alarm. What was happening to her? Why were her emotions running riot like this?

Slowly the truth began to dawn on her. And as it did, her eyes opened wide and she gave a great gulp.

'Oh, no!' she whispered, panic starting to build up inside her as a blaze of comprehension began to illuminate everything with terrifying clarity. 'You can't have—you really *can't* have——'

She gulped again, even harder. She had known for some time that Zack was having a turbulent effect on her body chemistry, but what she hadn't known—or, at least, had refused to admit to herself—was why. It was all becoming frighteningly clear now, though. Seeing Zack with Sam, seeing Sam kissing him, had jolted everything into place.

'But you *can't* have fallen in love with him,' Nell muttered to herself. 'You simply can't. Not in such a short time. And without knowing about it. You wouldn't do anything so crazy!'

He despises you, she reminded herself frantically. He thinks you're ambitious and self-centred, that you use people, that you'll do anything to get publicity to further your career—you don't even care if it's bad publicity. Nell gave a small groan as she realised she had actually encouraged him to think of her in that way. And everything she had done today had simply reinforced that opinion.

You've got to be wrong about this, she told herself with another faint groan. Keep on telling yourself that he's the last man on earth you want to get involved with, remember you're not ready for another relationship; there are a hundred and one reasons why it wouldn't—couldn't—work.

She slumped further down in the seat, and the sun blazed through the window, almost grilling her, but she didn't even notice its scorching heat. This hasn't happened, she kept stubbornly telling herself over and over. *It hasn't happened*.

She flicked back her damp hair almost in despair as she failed to convince herself. Didn't she ever learn? First she had got involved with Lloyd Kendrick, who had simply used her, and now Zack Hilliard was threatening to tear her apart emotionally all over again. What was the matter with her? How could she keep falling for men who were so wildly unsuitable?

You haven't fallen for him, she argued with herself with dogged determination. It's just—well, the two of you have been staying under the same roof, and you're pretty vulnerable at the moment. If you'd met him in normal circumstances, you probably wouldn't have given him a second look.

Except that was a lie, of course. Zack was the kind of man who always commanded second, third and fourth looks.

Nell closed her eyes because her head was whirling. Sleep for half an hour while you're waiting for Zack, she ordered herself. When you wake up again, you'll feel normal. You'll have forgotten about all this.

Except that she couldn't sleep, it was too hot. A couple of times she slid into a light, restless doze, but then her eyes would suddenly snap open again and she would feel horribly nervous and edgy. Then she would remember *why* she felt nervous and edgy, and she would groan for the umpteenth time.

By the time Zack finally returned, she was an almost total wreck. Wild-eyed, her hair unplaited and twisted into a dark tangle where she had kept running her fingers through it, and all her nerve-ends feeling positively raw.

As Zack got into the car, he shot a quick glance at her and frowned. 'Your face is very flushed. It probably wasn't a good idea to wait here in the car— it's too hot. You look as if you might have a touch of heatstroke.'

Yes, that was what it was, Nell told herself with a great surge of relief. Heatstroke! The way she felt was nothing to do with Zack, it was just too much sun— and probably too much wine. That third glass had gone to her head.

Zack started up the car and headed out of the city. The sun was no less bright as they reached the Tuscan hills, but somehow it seemed cooler. Nell felt some of the heat seeping out of her skin, and she began to breathe more easily. She really was feeling much better now. What had happened in Florence had been very odd—and disturbing—but her head had stopped spinning and her nerves were no longer fluttering wildly out of control. The heat and the wine, she told herself again—they had caused all those strange and rather terrifying feelings. She would be very careful not to combine the two again, in the future!

The farmhouse finally came into view, and she began to feel even more relaxed. She would have a shower, a meal and an early night. By morning, she was sure she would feel like her old self again.

They went inside, and, despite the heat of the late afternoon sun, the stone walls had kept the interior cool.

'I'm going straight up to have a shower,' she said, turning towards the stairs.

'Not just yet,' Zack said, moving in front of her and blocking her path.

Nell became very still. 'What—what are you doing?' she asked in a small voice.

'I think there are a couple of things I'd like to talk over,' he said, a dark glint appearing in his eyes.

'I don't think I want to talk about anything, thank you,' she said nervously.

'Not even about Sam? And the reason you ran away as soon as she appeared on the scene?'

'I didn't run away!' she denied. 'I simply went back to the car. I didn't think the two of you would want me around.'

'Why?' asked Zack levelly.

'Because most men like to be on their own when they've just been kissed by a beautiful blonde!'

'Yes, Sam is beautiful,' he agreed. 'But so are you,' he added in a softer tone. 'There's no need for you to be jealous.'

'I'm not jealous!' she lied vehemently.

'Then why behave the way you did?'

'I don't want to discuss this any more.'

'But I do,' said Zack, his blue gaze fixing on her face. 'I'm finding it very interesting.'

'Well, I'm not!'

'You don't want to know more about Sam? You don't want to know that we're old friends? That once, for a very short time, we were rather more than that, but it didn't work out, we were more comfortable as friends than lovers?'

'No, I don't want to know that,' Nell muttered.

'Then you also won't want to know that I provided Sam with the finance to set up her agency, renting out holiday homes in Tuscany. And that we meet up occasionally, to discuss problems and map out plans for the future.'

'I don't want to know that either.' Except that she did, of course. She wanted to know every single thing that went on in Zack's life.

'That kiss she gave me was simply a friendly kiss,' he went on. 'There was no need for you to go bright green with jealousy.'

Nell's brown eyes flashed. 'I've already told you that I wasn't jealous!'

Zack ignored her retort. 'You're old enough, intelligent enough, to know the difference between a kiss like that and the kisses I gave you.'

'They looked exactly the same to me,' she said stiffly.

'Then perhaps I'd better demonstrate the difference.'

Her stomach immediately lurched uncomfortably. 'I d-d-don't want to be kissed again,' she stuttered in alarm.

'Of course you do. Almost as much as I want to do it.'

Something about his tone of voice made Nell shiver right down to the very roots of her soul. She suddenly realised that this was getting to be a highly dangerous situation. Just how much of it could she cope with?

As much as she had to, she told herself sturdily. She would be all right; the effects of the heat and wine had worn off, and she had nothing to worry about. If Zack insisted on kissing her, it wouldn't be a problem. She could cope with it, she wasn't going to fall apart.

She straightened her shoulders and flicked back her long dark hair.

'I don't suppose I can *stop* you kissing me?' she challenged him, with far more bravado than she felt.

'Of course you can. You simply have to convince me that you really don't want me to do it.'

'I don't,' she said at once, lying with a fervour born of desperation.

He moved closer. 'I'm not convinced, Nell,' he said silkily.

Her heart was thundering away so fast that it seemed to shake every bone in her body. She started to back away from him, but then stopped. What was the use? She had enough experience to recognise when a man was absolutely determined to go through with something. And Zack, for some inexplicable reason of his own, looked as if nothing short of an earthquake would stop him carrying out his intention to kiss her.

Instead she stood quite still, and braced herself both mentally and physically. It won't take long, she tried to reassure herself. Probably just a few seconds. Definitely no more than half a minute. Then it will all be over.

She had closed her eyes, as if blotting out the sight of him would help her to get through it. When nothing happened, she slowly opened them again.

Zack was still standing very close, looking directly at her, and there was an expression on his face that she couldn't remember ever seeing before. Then he seemed to realise that she was looking back at him, and he shook his head abruptly, as if he wanted to clear some unwanted thoughts out of it.

All this waiting around was making Nell's nerves feel even more frayed. 'If you have to do this, then please get it over with quickly,' she said in a tight voice.

Zack's temper remained unruffled. She even thought she could see the shadow of his rare, wolfish smile touching the corners of his mouth.

'But I don't like to hurry,' he told her almost lazily. 'I like to make love slowly.'

Her brown eyes shot wide open in alarm. 'But you're not making love, you're only kissing me,' she gabbled in a voice that definitely *wasn't* steady any longer.

His grin broadened, stretching his mouth into a long, sensual line.

'Don't you think the two things are connected, Nell? If not, you must have had some very strange—and disappointing—kisses.'

'I've had a lot of kisses, and none of them was disappointing,' she insisted sturdily, although not altogether truthfully.

'I'm beginning to think that none of them was very exciting either,' Zack remarked thoughtfully.

'And you think yours will be?' she shot back at him. Then she immediately regretted saying that. It had sounded too much like a challenge—and she had the feeling that Zack very much enjoyed challenges.

'Perhaps this is a good time to find out,' he suggested, and moved swiftly towards her before she had the chance to say anything else.

She had been expecting a kiss like the one he had given her last time, hard and intense. She had even braced herself against it. The kiss he gave her was nothing like that, though. It was butterfly-soft, his mouth brushing with only the very gentlest of movements against her own, his tongue licking so lightly that she could scarcely feel it.

Nell hadn't been prepared for a kiss like that, and she was alarmed to find that she didn't seem to have any defences against it. There was something so disarming about that light touch; it knocked her completely off balance. She couldn't accuse him of being brutal, of using his superior male strength against her without a thought for her own feelings. She couldn't accuse him of anything at all—except arousing the oddest sensations in all her nerve-ends as his mouth drifted slowly onwards, and his tongue explored a little further, but oh, so delicately, causing her lips actually to quiver under its light touch.

Nell gave a small gulp. How would she feel if he touched her in the same way? If his hands danced over her body in the same intricate, delicate way?

A moment later she found out. His fingertips came to rest against the soft underswell of her breast, barely touching; she only seemed to know they were there because of the heat that flowed from them, burning gently against her skin. Then they edged upwards, slowly, very slowly, and she held her breath, she couldn't move, and then one finger—just one finger— touched the small, hard tip of her breast, only touched it, but a shaft of exquisite pleasure shot through her, followed by another, and then another, as that finger gently rubbed backwards and forwards, still with that tormenting lightness.

A deep shudder ran through her and she began to breathe again, although with light, unsteady breaths.

'See how nice it can be if you don't rush things?' Zack murmured.

'I'm not enjoying this,' Nell lied in a last desperate attempt to hold on to her sanity.

Zack merely smiled. Then he kissed her again.

This time the kiss wasn't so light, so controlled. And his hand swiftly, expertly slid under her blouse, under the thin cotton of her bra, as if he suddenly needed to feel the silky heat of her skin against his palm.

Nell knew this was the most frightening thing that had ever happened to her. She had been in this sort of situation before, but she had always felt she had

had some sort of control over it. She had always been able to stop it before it went any further than she had wanted it to.

Now, though, she wasn't sure she would be able to stop it at all. And not because of Zack, but because of *herself*. Something inside her was treacherously urging her to surrender to this man. She wanted more and more of the exquisite sensations that he could provoke with his mouth and his hands. But, more unnerving than that, she wanted to be with him, to know every single thing about him. She adored every inch of him, from the top of his dark head down to the tips of his toes. It was the reason why he could so easily arouse her, while most other men had only been able to make her feel rather inadequate because she couldn't respond to them with genuine, uninhibited feeling. It was also the most terrifying thing that had ever happened to her.

It's crazy to feel like this, she told herself shakily. He's never going to love you; he simply *wants* you. And if you let him know how much you want him back, then you're going to be in desperately serious trouble.

Zack lifted his head and looked at her, as if he could actually read her turbulently mixed-up thoughts.

'Confused?' he asked softly.

'No,' she muttered. That was a downright lie, of course—and she was usually so truthful!

'I am,' he said, to her astonishment. 'This doesn't seem to be working out quite the way I expected.'

'Then why won't you let me go?' Nell demanded with sudden fierceness. 'Then you won't be confused any more!'

'But I wouldn't be able to do this either,' Zack murmured, and bent his head and kissed her again.

Each kiss was a little more forceful than the last—and a little more devastating. One more, just one more, thought Nell in growing panic, and I'll melt away, and he'll be able to do exactly what he likes with me.

Just the thought of it was enough to make her shiver almost convulsively. Then, almost immediately, she shivered again. Zack felt her response and drew back slightly. Then his dark brows drew together in a faint frown.

'Cold?' he asked. His hand slid over her, causing her to shiver for a third time. 'But your skin's hot.'

'Sunburn,' Nell gabbled. 'I think I've got sunburn. It's making me go hot and cold.'

His frown deepened. 'Are you feeling ill?'

With relief, she realised he had given her an escape route. A chance to get away from him—if she wanted to.

You *do* want to, she told herself fiercely. Use your common sense! You can't possibly get involved with Zack Hilliard—it would be mad. She forcefully reminded herself that she wouldn't be able to face her family—or herself—if she went from one catastrophic relationship straight into another.

'I—I don't feel all that well,' she lied again, in a low voice. 'I've got a headache, feel a bit dizzy.'

Zack stepped back and his blue eyes fixed on her in a long scrutiny. 'Your face is far too flushed,' he said at last. 'It was very hot in Florence. You must have stayed out in the sun and the heat for too long.'

Nell knew very well that the flush that covered her skin hadn't been caused by the sun. Part of her longed to admit that. The other part—the sensible part—warned her to hang on to the subterfuge.

'You'd better go and lie down for a while,' said Zack, with another small frown.

'I think that's a good idea,' she mumbled. In fact, it was a *very* good idea! Her legs were still shaking gently from those kisses he had given her. She just hoped she could make it up the stairs.

'I'll get you a cool drink,' Zack went on. 'It's important to take in a lot of liquid if you've been out in the sun for too long.' He hesitated, then added, 'Look, I'm sorry about everything that's happened since we got back. If I'd known you weren't feeling well——'

'Would it have made any difference?' asked Nell in a stiff voice. 'You were just doing what so many men do—going after what *you* want, and not caring in the least if the other person wants the same thing or not.'

His eyes hardened a fraction. 'Are you telling me you didn't want those kisses?'

'Of course I didn't want them,' she forced herself to say. Another lie, of course—how many more was she going to tell, before this was over?

Zack's face became harder. 'I don't believe that,' he growled.

'Don't you mean you don't want to believe it?' she challenged him rashly. 'Do you think I can't fake a response to a kiss? But remember what I am—an actress. I'm also the girl who'll do anything for publicity. I might have decided it was worth deliberately trying to turn you on, now that I know you're also Jackson Paine, a man who can make the headlines with million-dollar contracts!'

She held her breath as his face became positively thunderous. 'If I thought for one moment——' he began in a grim voice. Then she saw him get a grip on his temper and force it back under control. The darkness slowly left his face, and his vivid blue gaze became less intense. 'No,' he said at last, more softly, as his eyes bored down into hers, 'I don't think you're a girl who fakes anything.'

'You can't be sure of that,' she said stubbornly.

The last of the tension left his face and his mouth relaxed. 'Yes, I can. If you'd really wanted me to stop kissing you, you wouldn't have bothered to fake anything, you'd simply have fought me tooth and nail.'

'I'm half your size. What would have been the point in fighting you?'

Rather disconcertingly, he suddenly grinned at her. 'No point at all. But you'd still have tried it.'

'I—I——' Nell tried hard to come up with a reason why she hadn't fought him. There was only one real explanation, though, but she would have died before telling him what it was. She was still trying to convince *herself* that it couldn't possibly be true.

'I wasn't feeling well,' she muttered at last in a subdued voice. 'The heatstroke——'

'Oh, yes, the heatstroke,' Zack said thoughtfully. 'It seems to have improved quite miraculously in the past couple of minutes.'

'I still feel hot and shaky,' Nell insisted.

'I'm sure you do,' he said silkily. 'But I don't think it's got anything to do with over-exposure to the sun.'

'You're so conceited!' she threw back at him. 'You can't possibly think it's got anything to do with those couple of kisses you gave me?'

There was a new light gleaming in his eyes, now. Nell saw it—and didn't like it. It signalled danger, although not of the physical kind.

'I'm going up to my room,' she went on, in a voice that she had meant to be very firm, but which came out with a distinct quiver. 'I intend to lie down until I feel better. Please don't disturb me.'

'How could I possibly disturb you?' murmured Zack, that gleam in his eyes brightening still further.

'Just don't—don't come near me,' she choked. Then she turned round and fled up the stairs, praying he wouldn't come after her.

He didn't—and Nell was horrified at the wave of disappointment that swept through her. Are you mad? she asked herself in disbelief. You manage to get away from him, and you're *disappointed*?

This was all getting completely out of hand. Perhaps her brain really had been addled by the sun, she told herself as she stripped off her crumpled clothes and stepped into the shower.

The warm water beat down on her, and it should have relaxed her, but it didn't. She finally got out of the shower feeling just as tense, and as she rubbed herself dry, she shivered a little because her skin still felt sensitive.

That was very worrying. Zack had touched her with just his fingers and the palm of one hand, but her skin was still reacting to that touch many minutes later. This was getting crazier and crazier, she muttered to herself.

Outside, it was growing dark. The hills were slowly vanishing into the dusk, and musky evening scents drifted in the open window. Nell told herself she should go to bed, get some sleep, and hope a little sanity had returned by the morning. She wasn't tired, though. And her room—in fact, the entire farm-house—suddenly felt claustrophobic. She needed fresh air, needed to feel the cool night breeze against her face, which was becoming uncomfortably flushed again.

She quickly pulled on a thin cotton dress and slid her feet into a pair of sandals. Her hair, still damp from the shower, hung loose down her back, drying into dark tendrils. Cautiously she opened the door and peered out. She certainly didn't want to run into Zack. She needed time on her own.

There was no sign of him. In fact, the farmhouse seemed silent and deserted. Nell gave a small sigh of relief and went soundlessly down the stairs.

She moved swiftly through the farmhouse, reached the back door, opened it and went out on to the terrace. Overhead, the stars were beginning to glitter brightly in the velvet-black sky. A half-moon hovered over the hills, and the trees were dark shadows around her, their leaves whispering faintly in the soft breeze.

Nell moved further into the garden. A narrow path led between the overgrown flowerbeds, and scent drifted up all around her as the flowers gently perfumed the night.

Slowly she began to relax. This was what she needed, to be on her own in tranquil surroundings. This was why she had come to the farmhouse, in the first place. Because she had desperately wanted to find a refuge, somewhere to lick her wounds after that awful episode with Lloyd Kendrick.

She realised, with a small jolt of surprise, that she hadn't even thought about Lloyd for a couple of days. Quite suddenly, everything that had happened to her because of him seemed completely unimportant.

'That's amazing,' she said out loud to herself, in astonishment.

'What's amazing?' murmured Zack's voice from just behind her.

Every nerve in Nell's body gave a violent jolt. She hadn't heard a single sound—he must have moved with absolute silence. She shakily turned round to face him. Even in the moonlight she could clearly see that a predatory glint lit his eyes. Like a hunting cat, she told herself with another jolt of alarm. And one that intended stalking its prey until it was finally forced to surrender.

'I—I came out here because I want to be on my own,' she said jerkily.

'No, you don't. It isn't good for people to be on their own.'

'You live here on your own,' Nell pointed out.

'Only because there's never been anyone I've wanted to bring with me. That's always been the problem,' Zack said softly. 'There's never been quite the right person. And I'd never settle for second best.'

'Well, I'm sure that I'm not the right person,' she muttered, turning her head away so that she wouldn't have to look into his eyes, those damned eyes that always seemed to see right through her.

'No, you're not,' he agreed. 'You're all the things that I hate and despise. At least, most of the time I think you are,' he added more softly. 'But just lately, there've been moments when I'm not so sure.'

'Would you still say that if I were short and fat and ugly?' she said just a little bitterly, only too aware how her stunning looks could affect men's judgement of her.

'But you're none of those things,' said Zack, his blue gaze fixing on her face and not moving away. 'You've got such delicate bones that I'm almost afraid to touch you. Long, glossy hair that would feel like silk if I wound it round my fingers. And deep, dark eyes that sometimes look so innocent it's impossible to believe you could ever have done anything deceitful or despicable.'

Nell swallowed very hard. She ached to tell him the truth about herself, but was too frightened. She wouldn't be able to bear it if he still didn't believe her, if there was still a small glimmer of doubt in his eyes.

'You're also very sexy,' he added in a sightly huskier tone.

'No, I'm not,' she muttered.

'Wrong, Nell. If you had any idea what you do to me, you'd——' He stopped, as if deciding he had already said too much. Instead his hand reached out and one finger traced a light path round her throat to the nape of her neck. 'Come back into the farmhouse with me,' he invited in a low, velvet voice.

How could she? When just the touch of that one finger was already causing devastation inside her?

'No,' she croaked, finding it incredibly hard to get out that one short word.

He didn't seem angry at her refusal. 'Why not?' he asked quietly.

'Because——' Her voice cracked completely, and she cleared her dry throat and tried again. 'Because I'm not interested in just—just sex.'

'Are you absolutely sure that's all this is?'

His softly spoken question caused more confusion inside her.

'Of course that's all it is,' she said a little desperately. 'You've already told me you want me, so what else could it possibly be?'

'I don't know,' Zack said thoughtfully. 'But I think I'd like to try and find out.' He slid his finger under her chin and forced her head up, so that she had to look directly into his brilliant eyes. 'Come into the farmhouse with me?' he invited again, holding her gaze with a merciless intensity.

Nell felt hypnotised by those eyes. They seemed to drain away the last of her fragile will-power.

Zack turned round and began to walk towards the farmhouse. And she found herself following him, as if she had never, ever had any choice in the matter.

CHAPTER EIGHT

INSIDE the farmhouse, it was dark. Nell hadn't switched on any lights as she had left it. And as they went back in, Zack left it in darkness.

What was it about the night? Nell asked herself shakily. People changed after dusk closed in around them; they did things they wouldn't have dreamt of doing in broad daylight.

Like going upstairs with Zack Hilliard. She still couldn't quite believe she was actually doing it. She kept telling herself she had to stop, turn around, run away, but her legs kept on carrying her unsteadily up the stairs.

When they reached the top, Zack turned to her.

'My room or yours?' he asked.

'N-neither,' she stuttered, somehow dredging up a small surge of resistance.

Even in the darkness she could see his eyebrows gently rise. And his eyes looked black, not blue. But they were still dangerous eyes.

'You've changed your mind?'

'I just d-don't think——' She tried to pull herself together and get out a coherent sentence. 'I don't think we should be here at all.'

'Of course we should,' Zack said calmly.

'We're not—I mean, we don't—there isn't——' She gave up babbling, and instead sighed softly. She

seemed to have reached the stage where she couldn't
string together half a dozen words that made any
sense. What was happening to her? No one had ever
been able to reduce her to a gibbering wreck before!

'Why don't you stop chattering and come with me?'
Zack suggested.

Somehow it was more of an order than a suggestion.
And before she could protest—or at least, *try* to
protest—he had shepherded her into the nearest room.
His room.

Nell gulped. This was all getting completely out of
hand. 'I think we should put on the light,' she
managed to get out.

'Why?' he asked, and, although she couldn't clearly
see his face in the darkness, she knew that faint wolfish
smile was beginning to touch the corners of his mouth.
'Have you forgotten what I look like?'

No, she didn't think she was ever going to forget
what he looked like. That dark hair, the sensual
mouth—and those blue, blue eyes.

He reached out and switched on the lamp beside
the bed. 'On the other hand,' he went on in a relaxed
tone, 'I think I would like to see you.'

He turned back to her, and Nell gulped again. She
wished the light had stayed off! In the darkness, she
hadn't been able to see the deep glitter in his eyes, or
the faint flush of colour along his cheekbones. And
although his tone might still be casual, there was absolutely nothing relaxed about his body. Every muscle
was taut, and there was a stillness about him that was
completely unnerving. She had seen that same stillness
in great cats—just before they pounced!

'I—I think this is a mistake,' she croaked. 'Anyway, I didn't mean to do this. I never meant to come up here.'

'How did you get here, then?' Zack challenged her softly. 'I don't remember dragging you up the stairs.'

'You made me walk through the door,' she accused nervously.

His mouth relaxed into a deeper smile. 'You didn't fight me. Or turn round and try to run away.'

She chewed her lip edgily. Now that she was in here, she didn't know how she was going to get out again. She knew she didn't even *want* to get out—and that was the most terrifying thing of all.

'Don't bite your lip,' Zack instructed, moving closer. 'Let me do it instead.'

'I don't want to be bitten!' she exclaimed in a panicky voice.

'Of course you do.' The wolfish smile vanished and something a lot more sensual took its place. 'Being bitten can be very nice, as long as it's done carefully—and gently.'

'I don't believe you.'

'Then I'd better give you a demonstration.'

She began to say a very definite no, but the sound was immediately muffled by his mouth. That was alarming, because she didn't even remember seeing him move. One moment he was standing a couple of feet away, and the next he was frighteningly close.

There wasn't very much time to worry over it, though, because by then he *was* biting her. Small, gentle nibbles that left her mouth slightly swollen, although not because of any bruising he had inflicted.

Zack raised his head and she could see that the glitter in his eyes had intensified.

'Like that?' he said softly.

Nell found it impossible to lie. She gave a small, jerky nod of her head.

'Good,' he went on, with satisfaction. 'I've the feeling we're going to discover a lot more things you like before this is over.'

His words made something inside her tremble almost violently. She felt as if she were standing on the edge of a deep, dangerous chasm—and she was about to fall into it.

His mouth returned to hers and she didn't seem to be able to do anything to stop it. She meant to protest—but didn't. Meant to keep her lips closed against him—but couldn't.

Experienced kisses from an experienced man. And Nell, who until now had thought she knew all about kissing, discovered she knew nothing at all.

His mouth and tongue explored, seemingly at leisure, and yet she was aware of the iron self-control he was exerting over himself, holding back and holding back, not wanting to rush her, not wanting to scare her.

Except that she was scared. Every single thing about this odd relationship they had scared her. She was even frightened of herself because of her intense reaction to this man. It had never happened to her before, not quite like this. It made everything that had happened between herself and Lloyd Kendrick pale into complete insignificance. She had thought she had been dazzled by Lloyd, but she had been completely wrong.

This was what it meant to be dazzled by someone. This feeling of utter helplessness, this terrifying lack of control over everything you felt for them.

Zack had still done nothing except kiss her. That didn't mean that nothing else had happened between them, though. The very air in the room seemed charged with a new, raw-nerved tension, overlaid with dark sensual undertones.

He released her mouth and took a step back. 'Will you undress for me?' he said softly.

Nell felt her hands obediently slide up to the small buttons at the neck of her dress. You can't do this, she told herself with a gulp. But her fingers were already unfastening the buttons, and the dress slid from her shoulders, slipped easily to the floor.

She had never done anything even remotely like this before. Yet, as Zack's intense blue gaze slid over her, she stood a little straighter, a little taller. Her breasts strained against the soft cotton of her bra. With one small movement she released the catch and the cotton fell away.

'Beautiful,' Zack said throatily. Then, more softly, 'Do you like it when I tell you you're beautiful?'

Numbly she nodded.

'Come here and let me touch you,' he invited softly.

She took a step forward, so that she was within reach of his hands, his clever hands that knew exactly how to caress and explore and arouse.

'Skin like silk,' he said appreciatively. His fingertips moved lightly across its soft texture, then he bent his head, so that his mouth could follow the same trail, his lips could taste her.

Nell shivered convulsively, but from pleasure, not from cold. He felt her reaction, and pulled her a little closer. Through the thin material of his shirt, she could feel the heat of his body. She knew very well that that heat was going to burn her, but there didn't seem to be anything she could do about it.

How could she feel like this about someone she had known for such a short time? She didn't know. She didn't even particularly care. Being with him was the only thing that was important.

Naked, except for a brief pair of panties, she stood within the circle of his arms and realised that this was the only place in the world that she wanted to be. That was another totally scary revelation. She began to feel that if one more new emotion crept up on her she would begin to crack apart under the strain.

'Nervous?' he asked, as he pushed back a long strand of her hair and his tongue licked gently at a particularly vulnerable spot at the base of her throat.

'Yes,' she croaked.

'Of me?'

'No,' she said in a low voice. And that was the truth. Everything about this situation made her nervous, except for Zack himself. Nell gave a small sigh. She didn't understand any of this. She really was very mixed up. She knew she needed time to think—but she also knew that Zack wasn't going to allow her that time.

He began to ease her towards the bed. She wanted to protest that she wasn't ready, but that would have been a lie, because she *was* ready. She could feel the impatience gathering in him, now, his self-control becoming harder to hold on to. His hands remained gentle, though, and there was nothing hurried about his movements. He had told her before that he liked to make love slowly, and she was beginning to realise that there could be an exquisite pleasure in not giving in immediately to the increasingly tumultuous feelings that he was coaxing from her.

His blue eyes fixed on her. 'Want to watch me undress?' he invited softly.

Nell swallowed hard. She tried to say yes, but it wouldn't come out, the sound became strangled in her suddenly dry throat.

Zack seemed to know exactly what she had meant to say, though. He slid off his shirt, and her gaze fixed with a touch of awe on the breadth of his shoulders, the powerful set of his chest, and the smooth texture of his tanned skin. Then he unzipped his jeans and, in easy movements, stepped out of them.

He was highly aroused. His arousal and his nakedness seemed perfectly natural, though, and when he drew her towards him again she didn't shrink back. An exhilarating lack of inhibition ran through her, and she realised that in the few days she had known him, he had forced her through the whole gamut of emotions. He had even made her reach the stage where she had wanted to run away from him. She didn't want to run away now, though. She wanted to stay very, very close—for ever.

Zack bent his head and kissed her again, but his kisses weren't so gentle, and neither was the touch of his hands. He was still holding her tightly against him, hot skin rubbing against hot skin and provoking yet more heat, but her closeness was breaking down his self-control. The musky scent of him swept over her; his hard, very male body imprinted itself against her. Then he raised his head and his blue eyes looked down at her with glittering brightness.

'Almost the point of no return, Nell,' he warned huskily.

The bed was just behind her. She slid down on to it and, a second later, he stretched out beside her.

'Willingly,' he said, still looking directly into her own darkened brown eyes. 'You must do this willingly.'

'I'm not telling you to go away,' she whispered.

Zack's mouth relaxed into an unexpected smile. 'No,' he agreed. 'Which in itself is a new and interesting experience!' His hand slid over the curve of her breast, then returned again, stayed this time, provoking fresh bursts of pleasure.

She knew her skin was as damp as his own, knew her heart was beating just as fast and erratically. When she touched him, he gave a small shudder, but her own body was shaking now as his hands moved more intimately, rubbed sensuously against her stomach, the curve of her hip, and the soft, soft skin of her thighs. Then they dipped deeper, touching inner warmth, so that pleasure began to roll over her in waves.

Already close, he eased his body still nearer so that there didn't seem to be an inch of him that wasn't locked against her. He murmured her name, gently caressed another intense surge of pleasure from her, then his fingers drifted away so that his body could ease inside her. And, like his nakedness, it seemed so natural, Nell was aware of only the very faintest sense of shock.

Relaxed and receptive, she responded at once as he moved against her. She was dimly aware that his self-control was falling apart, but *she* was falling apart as well, both of them tumbling down and down into a deep, deep well that was filled to the very brim with the most exquisite sensations. Then his movements quickened, his body began to tense, and she felt him try to hold back a little longer, but it didn't matter, she was already drowning in those sensations, and then he was drowning too—she heard him mutter her name in sudden surprise as if he couldn't quite believe the intensity of the pleasure that was making his body shake uncontrollably against hers.

Even when the last faint waves of pleasure had floated softly away, neither of them moved for a long time. Finally, though, Zack eased his weight away from her. Then he propped himself on one elbow and looked down at her.

He looked unexpectedly at a loss, as if for once he didn't know quite what to say or do. Nell reached out and gently touched him, and felt a light tension in his body, as if their lovemaking had left him not relaxed but rather disturbed.

Almost absently, he twined a lock of her dark hair around one of his fingers. Then he gave it a gentle tug. 'I'm beginning to find out more things about you than I ever expected to know,' he murmured at last.

'What kind of things?' asked Nell a little shyly.

He didn't answer, though. Instead his hand slowly stroked the sleek lines of her body, as if the silken texture of her skin against his fingertips calmed something inside him.

A little while later she became aware that he was becoming aroused again. She could feel the heat gently flowing back into her own skin, and felt his reaction as he too sensed it. When she tried to touch him, though, he gently held her hands away.

'Not yet,' he said huskily. 'I want to take it more slowly this time.'

Her eyes opened wide. 'More slowly than last time?'

'Oh, yes,' Zack promised throatily. 'Twice as long, twice as nice.' His hand was already teasing the peak of her breast back into a tender hardness.

And Nell lay back, let her gaze wander over him adoringly, and knew that this was the most amazing night of her entire life.

A long time later, they both slept. When Nell next opened her eyes, the sun was streaming in through the window. She felt deliciously relaxed and she lazily stretched her languid limbs.

She immediately touched the male body sprawled out next to her. Her brown eyes instantly opened even wider, because when she had first woken up her mind had been sleepily blank. She hadn't remembered a thing about last night.

She certainly remembered now, though! She shot out of the bed, as if Zack were red-hot and she would get burned if she touched him again.

Except that she had already been burned, she reminded herself shakily. Last night had confirmed a whole lot of things about herself that she would have been much happier not knowing. Very *uncomfortable* things—such as the way she felt about Zack.

She stared at him as he lay on the bed, still soundly asleep. His dark hair was tousled, his powerful body totally relaxed. Nell swallowed hard as she looked at him. This was a very inconvenient time to have fallen in love, she told herself, chewing her lip worriedly. And a very inconvenient man to have fallen in love *with*.

What was going to happen now? She didn't know. Didn't even dare think about it.

'Oh, this is a mess,' she muttered a little despairingly.

She began to back towards the door. She had to get out of here. Had to try and get this straightened out inside her mind before Zack woke up and began to confuse her all over again.

'Running out on me?' murmured Zack, without even opening his eyes.

'I'm—er—I'm going—I-I have to——'

One blue eye slid open and fixed on her. 'Stop gibbering,' he instructed. 'Go and shower, then get dressed. I'm going to Siena today. If you behave yourself, you can come with me.'

'I don't think I want to——' Nell began nervously, wishing he would close that eye again, because its intense blue gaze was already turning her legs to jelly.

'You're always telling me you don't want to do things,' he reminded her. 'But when it comes down to it, you actually want to do them very much.'

Nell immediately went bright scarlet, because she knew exactly what he was talking about!

Zack swung himself off the bed, and she swallowed hard. Even naked, he looked very imposing! Then she felt a *frisson* of apprehension run through her as she wondered what he was going to say—or do.

For a long time, he simply looked at her. He looked oddly indecisive, as if last night had confused him almost as much as it had her. Nell knew that was impossible, though. She just wasn't capable of reducing someone like Zack to a state of indecision.

'I suppose there are quite a few things we should talk about,' he said at last. 'But I don't think I'm in the right mood at the moment. Perhaps it would be better if we just relaxed for a few hours, spent some time together, perhaps got to know each other in a different kind of way.' His gaze remained fixed on her with a disconcerting intensity. 'I can't make my mind up about you, Nell,' he said more softly. 'Just when I think I know exactly who—and what—you are, you do something or say something that makes me wonder——'

'Wonder what?' she asked slightly breathlessly, as he suddenly stopped.

Zack rather abruptly shook his head. 'We'll talk about it later. Are you coming with me to Siena?'

She meant to say no, she really did. She knew very well that the more time she spent with him the more she was going to be entrapped by the turbulent feelings

he awoke in her. Instead, though, she heard herself
say a rather shaky yes. Then she turned and fled from
the room, heading for the refuge of the shower.

By the time she finally ventured downstairs, hair
freshly washed and gleaming, the light tan of her skin
glowing against her white cotton dress, she found Zack
was already waiting for her. His gaze drifted over her
appreciatively as she came towards him, and she found
herself feeling ridiculously shy.

'I'm—I'm ready,' she mumbled.

'You're the prettiest thing I've seen in the morning
for a very long time,' he said softly. 'Perhaps ever.'
And as the colour spread over her face, he added,
'*And* you can still blush. That's a rare talent
nowadays.'

'I'm hot, that's all,' she insisted in a flustered voice.
Then, in a hurry to change the subject, she asked,
'Why are you going to Siena?'

'Because it's the day of the Palio, and I've managed
to get tickets.'

'The Palio?' she repeated, slightly blankly.

'The bare-back horse race they hold in the great
square in the centre of the old part of Siena. Jockeys
are bribed, horses are doped, fights break out in the
crowd, it's noisy, passionate, corrupt and violent—a
great day out,' he added, with a grin.

'Does the jockey get a big prize if he wins?'

'The jockey isn't important,' Zack explained. 'They
often fall off—or are pushed off, by other jockeys.
It's the first horse past the post that wins, whether
it's got a rider or not. Each horse represents one of

the ancient districts of Siena, and the prize is the Palio
itself, a hand-painted silk banner.'

Nell was only half listening. She realised she was
finding the cadences of his voice slightly hypnotic. It
reminded her of—the heat began to sear through her
skin again as she realised that it reminded her of last
night, of the way his dark velvet voice had added to
his physical assault on her senses. She remembered
how, on his first night here at the farmhouse—and
that now seemed like half a lifetime ago!—she had
told herself that this was a man who knew all the secrets of the night. Well, she had certainly been right
about that! But what was she meant to do with all
these new feelings he had provoked in her? And how
did *he* feel? She had absolutely no idea—he hadn't
said, and she certainly hadn't dared to ask.

Nell decided she was going to go a little mad if she
kept on thinking about it. Zack was right, they needed
a break from the dark intensity of last night. In Siena,
surrounded by crowds of people, they would be able
to relax for a while.

'We'd better leave now or we might miss the race,'
she said, edging towards the door.

'It won't start until late in the afternoon,' Zack told
her. 'But there's a parade beforehand, with flag-
throwing and everyone dressed in medieval costume.'

'It sounds great,' said Nell, with rather forced en-
thusiasm. 'I can't wait to see it.'

'And of course, you'll feel safe surrounded by all
those people,' Zack commented, one dark eyebrow
twitching, as he followed her out.

She decided not to answer. She certainly wasn't going to admit that she didn't feel safe when they were alone together! She did hurry out to the car, though, diving inside and letting out a silent sigh of relief as Zack started up the engine and drove off.

It wasn't a long drive. They soon reached the suburbs of Siena and joined the long stream of cars crawling through the streets. Just as they reached the ancient city walls, a parking space miraculously appeared and Zack expertly manoeuvred the car into it.

'No point in trying to take the car any further,' he said. 'We'll walk from here.'

The old city seemed to be a maze of narrow lanes, bridged by stone arches. The rose-coloured stone of the buildings all around glowed in the sunlight, and Nell caught glimpses of even narrower alleyways winding in and out the jumble of houses, churches and palazzos.

A steady stream of people were all heading in the same direction. Some were obviously tourists, but a lot were young Italians, wearing coloured rosettes and bright sashes across their chests. They were noisy but cheerful, and excitement hummed in the air. Nell could sense it, but resisted its pull. After last night, she wasn't ready for any more excitement for a while!

'With all these crowds, we could easily get separated,' Zack murmured in her ear. 'Want to hold my hand?'

But Nell had already decided she wanted to avoid physical contact with him for the next few hours. That was something else she wasn't ready for, not until she had got a few things straightened out inside her head.

Anyway, it could so easily get out of hand—look what had happened last night! And although she kept telling herself she was safe with all these people around, those shadowy dark alleyways were never too far away. What if Zack tightened his grip on her hand, whipped her down one of the alleyways, then began kissing her, slid those clever fingers of his over her——?

Despite the heat, she gave a small shiver. She felt horribly vulnerable, and rather lost. If he came too close, then she really didn't think she was going to be able to cope with this at all.

'No, thank you,' she told him politely, 'I don't want you to hold my hand.'

His blue gaze fixed on her thoughtfully. 'Scared of me this morning?'

'I just don't want—I'm not ready——'

'I always know when you're nervous,' Zack said with a grin. 'You can never manage to finish a sentence.'

'I'm not nervous,' she denied, praying that her voice wouldn't crack and give her away.

'If it makes you feel any better, there are quite a few things *I* haven't managed to sort out yet.'

It didn't make her feel any better at all, because he could so easily sort them out in the wrong way. All he had to do was to decide that he had been right about her all along, that she *was* an over-ambitious and self-centred publicity-seeker, and that would be it. He would turn his back on her and walk away. And Nell knew he had the will-power to do it.

The lane they had been following opened out into a small, shadowed courtyard, then everyone surged through an opening on the other side and Nell blinked as she was hit by a surge of light and noise. They had come right out into the Campo, which was actually more of a circle than a square, and dominated by the great bell tower of the Palazzo at the far side. Brightly coloured banners and decorations hung from all the buildings that ringed the square, and fluttered from the balconies. People lucky enough to have a seat on one of the balconies would have the best view of all. The next best seats were in the tiers of wooden grandstands that ringed the outside of the square. In front of them was the racetrack itself, covered with golden sand, while the centre of the square would eventually be crammed with thousands and thousands of people, all jostling to see the race.

'Does everyone have to have a ticket?' asked Nell, diverted from all her problems by the noisy, colourful scene in front of her.

'Tickets are only sold for the grandstand seats. I've managed to get a couple, though. Everyone else just pushes into the centre of the square, then fights for a good view. It can get very rough,' Zack warned. 'The crowds can go wild during the race, and it's often chaos afterwards, with everyone either rushing to see the winning horse or trying to beat up the jockeys who lost.'

'It all sounds very violent,' she said doubtfully.

'It is,' Zack agreed. 'For the rest of the year, the Sienese are very law-abiding citizens. But, as I've told you, each horse represents a district of Siena, and everyone passionately wants *their* district to win the race. Perhaps we're all capable of a degree of violence when we're after something we really want,' he added, his blue gaze resting on her.

Nell shivered lightly. Was that a warning? Just how far would Zack go to get something he wanted? Or to get rid of something—or someone—he decided he *didn't* want?

He slid his fingers through hers, and she shivered a second time, although for a very different reason.

'If I don't hold your hand you're going to get swept away by the crowd,' he told her. 'And I don't want to lose you.'

Did he mean he didn't want to get parted from her here, in Siena? Or that he intended to hold on to her for a great deal longer than that?

Nell realised there were dozens and dozens of questions that she needed answers to. But the noise in the great square was rising now to the pitch where she could barely hear herself speak. The questions were going to have to wait until later.

Zack shouldered his way easily through the crowds massing in the square, towing her along in his wake. A few minutes later they were sitting on a hard wooden bench in one of the stands, with the great circle of golden sand where the horses would race spread out just a few feet in front of them. Nell was glad to see that strong, padded barriers protected them from the flying hoofs of the horses. She was also glad that she and Zack weren't crammed into the middle of the square. The crowds there were jammed in so tightly that when someone fainted from the heat and crush they had to be handed over the heads of the other spectators to first-aid posts at the edge of the Campo.

'Why did you get *two* tickets?' she asked him, almost shouting at him to make herself heard. 'You couldn't have known you were going to bring me.'

'I was going to invite Sam,' Zack said casually.

Just the mention of Sam's name brought back all the old pangs of jealousy. Nell was highly alarmed at how intense they still were.

'I suppose Sam was too busy to come, so I'm just a substitute,' she said a little indignantly.

'I can't imagine you being a substitute for anything,' Zack said drily. 'You're an original, Nell. Whoever and whatever you really are, you're certainly like no one else. The parade's starting,' he went on. 'We might as well sit back and enjoy it. It'll be quite a while yet before the actual race.'

But Nell found it hard to concentrate on the long, highly colourful procession, with everyone dressed in medieval costumes. The flags of all the districts of Siena were paraded, then the banners were tossed high into the air, their brilliant colours flashing in the sunlight as they spun round and round before coming back to rest in the skilful hands of the throwers.

The heat, the noise, the excitement, gradually built to fever pitch. The sheer intensity of it made Nell feel slightly dizzy—it was almost too much on top of everything else that had happened in the last twenty-four hours. Then it was time for the race itself, and the entire square went crazy. The horses lined up and the jockeys in their jewel-bright costumes, with the emblem of the district they represented emblazoned across their back, clung to the bare-backed horses.

As the race finally began, the entire square erupted explosively into new heights of noise and passionate emotion. The horses careered round, hoofs flying wildly, their jockeys jostled and elbowed each other, fighting for the front position, a couple fell off and the riderless horses galloped on, kicking up great sprays of sand as they flew round.

Three laps of the square, it was all over in a minute and a half, but even when the race was finished the wild excitement didn't die down. Crowds surged round the winning horse, yelling and cheering, losing jockeys ran for their life as they were chased by enraged spectators who had supported and backed the losers, and fights began to break out in the centre of the square.

'Time to leave,' said Zack, getting up and hauling Nell to her feet at the same time. 'Emotions run very high on the day of the Palio. Things can sometimes get out of hand, and I don't want to see you hurt.'

He forced his way easily through the thronging mass of people, past the groups of cheering supporters of the winning horse, and others who glowered darkly, their own horses having lost. Nell still felt dazed by the sheer uproar, the heat, and the intensity of emotion that had filled the square during the race. Yet something inside her had responded to that excitement. Her skin was hot and a little damp—the blood beat much faster in her veins. And she could feel the answering heat that radiated from Zack's own body, where their hands were linked she could feel the fast beat of his pulse.

If they went back to the farmhouse in this heightened state of emotion, what was going to happen?

She already knew the answer to that question, though, and just thinking about it sent a fresh flare of heat through her. This man aroused dark, hot emotions that she hadn't even known she was capable of feeling. A wild exhilaration that half frightened her and yet made her feel incredibly alive.

His grip on her hand tightened, as if he knew very well the thoughts shooting through her head. He began to walk faster, and Nell scurried along, to keep up with him. Neither of them said a word, but she knew very well that they were heading straight back to the car—then to the farmhouse—then to bed . . .

They were out of the square now, and heading down one of the narrow side streets. Shadowed by the tall buildings on either side, it was very slightly cooler, and yet the heat inside her didn't die down. Instead it seemed to intensify. Nell felt as if she were burning up from an intense mixture of love and desire.

Aware of little except the turmoil inside her and the hard, heated grip of Zack's hand, she didn't even notice the group of tourists approaching from the other direction. As they drew level, one of the women suddenly looked at Nell, said something to the person next to her, and another pair of eyes swivelled round to fix on her face.

A murmur went through the group, and their voices at last began to reach Nell.

'Is it her?'

'That girl who dumped him, a real little bitch——'

'She's prettier than she looked in the newspapers.'

'Perhaps we could get an autograph? I mean, I don't really want it, but it would prove to everyone back home that we really did see her.'

'I saw her film, and it was rubbish. I shouldn't think she'll get another part, and serve her right!'

'You can see from her face that she's the cool type, only out for what she can get.'

'I feel sorry for Lloyd Kendrick, getting involved with someone like her. But I'm still going to try and get her autograph.'

Nell had been listening to it all in sheer disbelief. As a couple of the women began to stride purposefully towards her, though, she realised that her worst nightmare really was happening—she had been recognised, she had suddenly become public property, someone people could openly abuse. All that bad publicity was still following her around. She desperately began to wonder if she was ever going to be free of it.

The group of tourists were still staring at her, and panic suddenly swirled through her. As the autograph-hunters got closer, she turned round and began to run, fleeing along the narrow, shadowed street, with no clear idea of where she was going except that she had to *get away*.

She had the awful feeling that she was going to be running for the rest of her life.

CHAPTER NINE

NELL had no idea how she eventually found her way back to the car. She had thought she was just running haphazardly, but then the city walls were in front of her and there was the car, just where they had left it. She went to yank open the door, then gave a yell of frustration. Zack had the keys!

'Are these what you want?' enquired Zack's voice from just behind her. Nell turned round and saw he was dangling the keys in front of her.

'Where did you come from?' she demanded.

'I've been just a few yards behind you all the way.'

'I thought——' Then she stopped abruptly.

'What did you think?' he asked, his blue eyes studying her keenly.

'That you wouldn't want to be seen anywhere near me,' she said in a low voice. 'Not after those people had recognised me.'

'Why did you run away?'

She suddenly glared at him. 'I'd have thought that was fairly obvious! Didn't you hear what they were saying about me?'

'I heard. But you don't run from people like that.'

'That's easy for you to say. They weren't talking about you. You don't know what it's like!'

'I know,' Zack said in a much grimmer tone, and Nell suddenly remembered what had happened to his father. The blaze of publicity must have spread to include Zack, as Hilliard's son. He certainly *did* know what it was like.

'Sorry,' she muttered, 'I forgot.'

'It doesn't matter. Get into the car. We'll go back home.'

Suddenly bone-tired, Nell slumped into the seat beside him. The city of Siena was soon left behind, and another golden sunset lit the Tuscan hills as the car sped onwards. The sky was bathed in colour, and the very air seemed to shimmer with gold light. Swallows darted overhead in their familiar chase after evening midges, the stone walls of old farmhouses glowed in the amber rays of the sinking sun, and the hills rolled gently into the distance, their outline becoming smudged as the light slowly faded.

By the time they reached the farmhouse, dusk was settling over the countryside. Nell went straight inside, but Zack remained standing in the doorway.

'Will you be all right on your own for a while?' he asked. 'I promised Signora Ginelli that I'd call in some time today, to take a look at her car. She's been having trouble getting it started.'

'I'll be fine. In fact, I'd like some time on my own.'

'I thought you might,' he said quietly. Then he added warningly, 'But when I get back, there are some things we're going to have to talk about. There's a lot of unfinished business between us, Nell.'

She didn't really want to think what that unfinished business might be. He might want to tell her it was time for her to go. That he didn't want to get involved any further with someone who was pointed at and discussed in the street, who couldn't show her face in public without attracting attention.

The farmhouse seemed very silent after he had gone. Nell wandered restlessly from room to room, unable to settle, unable even to think straight. She had thought she wanted to be on her own, but now Zack had left she realised she didn't want to be on her own at all. She didn't like it when he wasn't around, didn't even want to think that soon she might have to face life without him at all.

When she heard a car pull up outside, she gave a great sigh of relief. He had come back! He must have decided to leave Signora Ginelli's car until another day. Then she bit her lip apprehensively. But perhaps he had come to tell her things she didn't want to hear.

Whatever he's got to say, you can take it, she told herself staunchly. She lifted her head and walked firmly towards the door. As she opened it, she saw a tall figure in the darkness. Then the figure stepped into the pool of light spreading out from the entrance hall, and Nell caught her breath. It wasn't Zack. It was Lloyd Kendrick!

For a moment she thought she was hallucinating. The emotional roller-coaster she had been riding lately had finally affected her mind. Then Lloyd gave his familiar sexy grin, and Nell knew he was actually here in person.

'I had a hell of a job finding you,' he said, as he walked up to her. 'You certainly picked a good place to hide away!'

'I wouldn't have needed to hide if you hadn't told all those lies about me,' she retorted, still shaken by the sight of him. 'Go away, Lloyd! I don't want to see you or speak to you!'

'But that's why I'm here,' he said disarmingly. 'I want to explain. And to apologise.'

'Apologise?' Nell exploded. 'You could keep on saying you're sorry for the rest of your life, and it still wouldn't put things right!'

'But I didn't know the whole thing was a publicity set-up. I felt very badly about it when I found out, Nell.' He smiled at her, the same easy smile that looked so good on film. 'Please let me come in and explain.'

She didn't want to let him inside the house, but somehow she found herself standing aside so that he could saunter in. She followed him into the sitting-room, and Lloyd looked around appreciatively. 'This is very nice. I wish I could stay here with you for a while.'

'You can't,' she said shortly. 'And you were lying a moment ago—you knew from the very start that our so-called "love affair" was totally phoney. You didn't want me, you wanted publicity for the film. Your agent told me so.'

'I've changed agents,' Lloyd said lightly. 'He gave me bad advice, set up deals I knew nothing about. Believe me, Nell, I wouldn't do anything to hurt you.'

'That's why you were making love to another girl at the end-of-filming party?' she retorted. 'Why you told the national Press that I'd walked out on you, that I'd only been using you to further my career?'

'I feel badly about that as well,' Lloyd said earnestly. 'But I was totally drunk at that party. It's no excuse, I know, but everyone does things they regret when they're drunk. And then my agent kept on at me, said it wouldn't be good for my image if everyone knew the real reason you'd left. I panicked, Nell, I admit it. My career had hit a downward curve, and I was absolutely desperate to revive it. I'd already had two recent flops, that film *had* to succeed or I'd have been branded a loser. And once that happens, you're out. The film itself had turned out all right, but I knew it wasn't going to set the box office alight. It needed publicity, *I* needed publicity.'

'And you used me to get it,' she said bitterly.

'It was publicity for you, as well,' Lloyd pointed out. 'Your face and your name are well known now.'

Nell looked at him in disbelief. 'Do you really think I want to be well known for walking all over someone to further my career? For being an over-ambitious, unfeeling bitch?'

He looked unconcerned. 'It doesn't really matter whether the publicity's good or bad. A few more weeks and everyone will have forgotten it. But they'll remember your name.'

'I don't want to be remembered,' she retorted.

'Of course you do,' he said coaxingly. 'It's what it's all about, Nell. It's why you became an actress in the first place. And now I've got my apology over and done with, I've got some exciting news for you.'

Nell shook her head in amazement. He really did think that giving her his charming, sexy smile and saying he was sorry made everything all right.

Lloyd was already talking again, though. 'They're talking about a sequel, Nell. That publicity's beginning to work—more and more people have been going to see the film over the last couple of weeks; it looks like it's going to turn out a hit after all. So they want to do a follow-up.'

'A follow-up?' she repeated, rather numbly.

'The film ended where your character walked out on me. They don't want to leave it there, though; they want to make a second film where we get back together again.'

Nell was finally beginning to realise why Lloyd was here, why he had gone to the trouble of tracking her down. And it had very little to do with apologising for his behaviour!

'I think it'll work,' he was going on enthusiastically. 'With a good script and a first-rate director, we can pull it off.'

'And perhaps some more publicity would help?' Nell suggested. 'If our real-life affair began again—just as it does in the film—that would promote a lot of interest, wouldn't it?'

'You're finally getting the hang of how the publicity machine works,' Lloyd said eagerly. 'I knew you would—you're a girl who knows how to look after your own interests.'

'Oh, yes,' said Nell in a dangerously calm voice, 'I know how to look after my own interests. That's why I want you to get out of this house right now. That's why I never want to see you again, or hear any mention of a follow-up film. And that's why I'm going to sue you if one more lie about me appears in the Press.'

The look on Lloyd's handsome face might almost have been comical, under different circumstances.

Then his features hardened. 'You're going to do this film, Nell,' he warned. 'And you're going to go along with every publicity stunt we dream up. If you don't, I'll make very sure you never work in the industry again.'

'You haven't got that much power,' she said scornfully. 'You're a second-rate actor who relies too much on your looks, Lloyd. And you're a fifth-rate human being.'

'You little——!' He raised his hand, as if to hit her. Nell instinctively flinched, but before Lloyd could make another move towards her a tall figure came hurtling through the doorway, hauled him away from her, and then a clenched fist knocked him halfway across the room.

Nell stared first at Lloyd, sprawling on the floor in an ungainly heap. Then she stared at Zack, who was standing there with a face as black as thunder.

'Where—where did you come from?' she gulped.

'I was halfway down the road when a car passed me going the other way,' he said grimly. 'Since the road only leads to the farmhouse, I came back, to make sure you were all right. When I realised it was Kendrick, I was about to leave you alone together. I thought you might even have invited him here. Then I began to listen to your conversation, and it was so interesting that I stayed.'

'You heard all of it?' she queried, her eyes opening wide.

'Every single word.' His own eyes were almost black with rage. 'He wasn't content with ruining your life once, so he could get publicity for his damned film. He came here to persuade you to do it all over again!'

Lloyd stirred on the floor, then gave a faint groan. Zack immediately moved towards him.

'What are you going to do?' Nell asked nervously. She had never seen Zack in this kind of mood before.

'I thought I might beat him to a pulp!'

Lloyd immediately gave a frightened yelp. 'Not my face! You mustn't damage my face!'

'Why not?' demanded Zack relentlessly. 'The damage you did to Nell was much worse and longer lasting.'

'Please—I'll do anything,' Lloyd begged in a desperate voice.

Zack loomed over him, powerful and intimidating. 'Anything?' he repeated.

'Anything at all!'

'Such as writing—and signing—a statement which admits you lied to the Press, and you fabricated that entire story about Nell to get publicity for your film?'

'If I do that my career will be ruined,' Lloyd moaned.

'Blame the whole thing on your agent,' Zack advised. 'My guess is that he devised most of it anyway. You don't have the brains.' He walked over to the bureau in the corner, took out a pen and a couple of sheets of paper, then hauled Lloyd to his feet and sat him down at the table.

'Start writing,' he instructed. 'Put everything down, and do it fast. I don't like having you under my roof. I want you out of here.'

Lloyd began scribbling at top speed. Nell watched in amazement. She could hardly believe that any of this was really happening.

Just minutes later, Lloyd scrawled his signature at the bottom of the sheet. Zack skimmed through it, and nodded in satisfaction.

'That explains everything very succinctly. Now, I think you'd better leave before I change my mind about ruining your pretty face.'

Lloyd had probably never moved so fast in his life. Seconds later they heard his car revving up and then shooting off down the road.

'Would—would you really have beaten his face to a pulp?' asked Nell with a loud gulp.

'Of course not.' Zack suddenly grinned. 'But he didn't know that, did he? He believed me.'

'*I* believed you,' she said, relaxing just a fraction.

His grin broadened. 'Then perhaps I ought to give up writing and become an actor. And talking of careers——' he held the sheet of paper out towards her '—this should help to revive yours. If nothing else, it should cut down the unpleasant publicity and revise people's opinions of you.'

'I don't know what to say,' she said in a low voice.

'You needn't say anything at all. I'm the one who should be doing the talking. I took all that publicity at face value, I didn't want to hear your side of the story—and probably wouldn't have believed you, if you'd tried to tell me. Like Lloyd, I owe you a very big apology. The only difference is, I hope you'll accept mine. There's no real reason why you should,' he added. 'In my own way, I'm almost as bad as

Lloyd. You came here looking for some peace, a respite from everything that had happened to you, and instead you found me. I bullied you, I forced you to do things you didn't want to do, and I accused you of being a lot of things that you're not, and never were. If you had any sense, you'd follow Lloyd right out that door.'

'But I don't want to go anywhere,' Nell said at once.

'It would be in your own best interests to go. I'm not an easy man to live with, and I probably never will be.'

'No, you're certainly not easy,' she agreed wryly. 'But I'm beginning to get used to you. Anyway, my two weeks isn't up yet,' she reminded him, with the beginnings of a grin.

'I was planning on keeping you here a lot longer than that.'

'You—you were?'

'If you want to stay, of course.'

'You know very well I want to stay! I think you've known it longer than I have.' Then her face became more sober. 'There's something I want you to know. It's about Lloyd. I know that while we were filming, our so-called love affair was all over the papers. But I never—well, I didn't——' She took a deep breath and finally managed to blurt it out. 'I never went to bed with him.'

'Of course you didn't,' Zack said calmly.

His immediate acceptance of her statement made the breath catch in her throat. 'You believe me?' she said in a rather odd voice.

'You wouldn't lie about something like that. Anyway, you've got more sense than to go to bed with a loser like Lloyd Kendrick.'

'I was stupid enough to get involved with him in the first place. I went out with him willingly enough, and I even enjoyed all the attention we got from the Press,' Nell admitted shamefacedly.

'Anyone can be dazzled for a while when they're suddenly pushed into the limelight. He might even have persuaded you as far as the bedroom door. But that's as far as you'd have gone, Nell. You were never going to take that final step.'

'I took it with you!' she blurted out.

Zack suddenly smiled, and the last of the darkness left his eyes. 'That was different.'

'*How* was it different?'

'I don't think you need me to tell you that,' he said in a much lazier voice. 'Although if you come a little closer, I'll show you.'

But Nell still hung back. 'There's still the problem of the publicity,' she warned. 'If you give Lloyd's statement to the Press, they're going to get interested in the story all over again.'

To her amazement, Zack gave an unconcerned shrug. 'All right, so it happens. Do you think I can't handle something like that?'

'But you like your privacy—you even write under an assumed name so that the Press and public won't bother you,' she wailed.

'I like to be able to travel around unrecognised,' he agreed. 'But if the Press are hanging around for a while, I can certainly cope with the situation. And if they get *too* close, I'll make sure they don't enjoy the experience,' he added with a low growl. When Nell didn't reply, he looked at her. 'You've gone very quiet. Suddenly run out of words?'

'I don't think I know what else to say,' she admitted a little helplessly.

'You could try telling me you love me.'

'You—you don't *know* that,' she spluttered.

'Of course I know it,' he said calmly. 'A girl like you doesn't jump into bed with someone she's only known for a few days unless she's been bowled over by a whole truckload of very strong feelings.'

'I didn't jump,' Nell said a little stubbornly.

'I certainly didn't force you,' he pointed out.

'Well—no——'

'And I don't think you'd try to put up much of a fight if I decided to do the same thing all over again,' he added softly.

'Are you——?' Nell cleared her suddenly dry throat and tried again. 'Are you thinking of doing something like that?' Her voice came out as a nervous squeak. And her pulses gave a quick, hard thump as Zack casually moved nearer.

'I think about it all the time,' he said, his mouth relaxing into a wicked smile. 'And I've the feeling I'm going to go on thinking about it for the rest of my life.'

'The rest of your life?' she repeated, her brown eyes mirroring her amazement.

'What did you think? That I simply wanted someone I could have some fun with for the rest of the summer?'

'I—I'm not sure what I thought,' she said quite truthfully. Then she gave a small sigh. 'These last few days have been so very confusing.'

'They certainly have,' Zack agreed with some feeling. 'I don't think I've ever been hit by so many emotions in such a short space of time. I've been angry with you, I've wanted you, I've despised you and then despised *myself* because I couldn't stop myself getting involved with you. And then I realised I'd fallen in love with you, and that really knocked me off my feet.' He suddenly ran his fingers through his dark hair. 'Is any of this making any sense?'

'I think it's beginning to make sense to me,' said Nell, starting to relax just a fraction.

'Then come over here and kiss me, touch me, until I can make sense of it too,' he invited throatily.

She went, without any more protests. What was the point in fighting it any longer? She was drawn to this man by something so powerful that she was never going to have any hope of resisting it.

His kisses were deep and intense, his hands strong and possessive as they moved over the already familiar softness of her body.

A long time later, she raised her head and looked at him. 'Now I'm confused all over again,' she said breathlessly.

'Good,' he murmured. 'I like it when you're confused. I think I'll spend the rest of my life making sure your head's in a complete spin.'

'That's the second time you've mentioned the rest of your life,' Nell said in a low voice.

'Why not? This is going to be a long-term relationship, isn't it?'

'How do you know that?'

'I know,' Zack said with utter confidence. And Nell believed him.

'What are we going to do now?' she asked a little shyly.

His finger thoughtfully traced the outline of her breast, lingering appreciatively for a while on the small, hard peak.

'Short-term or long-term?'

'Both,' she said, giving a small shudder as his finger continued on its trail of exploration.

'Long-term, we can either stay in Tuscany for the rest of the summer, or we can go back to London and face the Press, get it over with. I've got to get some work done on my next book——' His hand slid beneath the thin cotton of her dress. 'Only I'll probably not get very far if you keep distracting me,' he went on more huskily, his fingertips rubbing lightly against the soft, warm inner skin of her thigh. 'You'll have to explain to my publisher exactly why I couldn't meet his deadline. And if you want to get back to work, that's fine with me, I'm quite happy to have a working wife. As a matter of fact, I've got some contacts who might be able to help. They'll judge you by your ability and talent, and ignore all that rubbish that was written about you in the Press.'

'Working *wife*?' Nell echoed in utter astonishment.

'We're talking about long-term plans,' he reminded her in a relaxed voice. 'And now that I've found what I've been looking for most of my adult life, I've no intention of letting you go. You'd better get used to that idea.'

Nell found she had absolutely no problem getting used to it.

'And—and short-term plans?' she asked breathlessly.

His finger stroked softly, intimately, producing a small, insistent ache of pleasure.

'Short-term, there are a couple of things I want you to do. First, I want you to admit that you love me.'

'I love you,' Nell said obediently. Then, as his dark brows drew together warningly, she said much more fervently, 'I *do* love you.'

'That's better,' he growled softly. At the same time, the heat radiating from his body intensified.

'What else do you want me to do?' she asked, her brown eyes beginning to sparkle.

Zack began to murmur in her ear, making her first blush, then throw back her head and laugh in sheer happiness.

This was absolutely mad, she told herself, falling so completely head over heels for someone she had only known a few days. But it was the most delicious madness she had ever known. And she knew she was going to love this man, marry this man—this stranger, who wasn't a stranger at all—and then spend the rest of her life getting to know every single thing about him.

Love is in the Air...

Mills & Boon have commissioned four of your favourite authors to write four tender romances.

Guaranteed love and excitement for St. Valentine's Day

A BRILLIANT DISGUISE	-	Rosalie Ash
FLOATING ON AIR	-	Angela Devine
THE PROPOSAL	-	Betty Neels
VIOLETS ARE BLUE	-	Jennifer Taylor

Available from January 1993   PRICE £3.99

Mills & Boon

*Available from Boots, Martins, John Menzies, W.H. Smith,
most supermarkets and other paperback stockists.
Also available from Mills & Boon Reader Service, PO Box 236,
Thornton Road, Croydon, Surrey CR9 3RU.*

THE PERFECT GIFT FOR MOTHER'S DAY

Mills & Boon

HAPPY
MOTHER'S
DAY

Specially selected for you –
four tender and heartwarming
Romances written by popular
authors.

LEGEND OF LOVE -
Melinda Cross

AN IMPERFECT AFFAIR -
Natalie Fox

LOVE IS THE KEY -
Mary Lyons

LOVE LIKE GOLD -
Valerie Parv

Mills & Boon

Available from February 1993   Price: £6.80

*Available from Boots, Martins, John Menzies, W.H. Smith,
most supermarkets and other paperback stockists.
Also available from Mills & Boon Reader Service, PO Box 236,
Thornton Road, Croydon, Surrey CR9 3RU.
(UK Postage & Packing free)*

Next Month's Romances

Each month you can choose from a wide variety of romance with Mills & Boon. Below are the new titles to look out for next month, why not ask either Mills & Boon Reader Service or your Newsagent to reserve you a copy of the titles you want to buy — just tick the titles you would like and either post to Reader Service or take it to any Newsagent and ask them to order your books.

Please save me the following titles:		Please tick	√
AN OUTRAGEOUS PROPOSAL	Miranda Lee		
RICH AS SIN	Anne Mather		
ELUSIVE OBSESSION	Carole Mortimer		
AN OLD-FASHIONED GIRL	Betty Neels		
DIAMOND HEART	Susanne McCarthy		
DANCE WITH ME	Sophie Weston		
BY LOVE ALONE	Kathryn Ross		
ELEGANT BARBARIAN	Catherine Spencer		
FOOTPRINTS IN THE SAND	Anne Weale		
FAR HORIZONS	Yvonne Whittal		
HOSTILE INHERITANCE	Rosalie Ash		
THE WATERS OF EDEN	Joanna Neil		
FATEFUL DESIRE	Carol Gregor		
HIS COUSIN'S KEEPER	Miriam Macgregor		
SOMETHING WORTH FIGHTING FOR	Kristy McCallum		
LOVE'S UNEXPECTED TURN	Barbara McMahon		

If you would like to order these books in addition to your regular subscription from Mills & Boon Reader Service please send £1.70 per title to: Mills & Boon Reader Service, P.O. Box 236, Croydon, Surrey, CR9 3RU, quote your Subscriber No:... (If applicable) and complete the name and address details below. Alternatively, these books are available from many local Newsagents including W.H.Smith, J.Menzies, Martins and other paperback stockists from 12th February 1993.

Name:...

Address:...

....Post Code:...........................

To Retailer: If you would like to stock M&B books please contact your regular book/magazine wholesaler for details.

You may be mailed with offers from other reputable companies as a result of this application. If you would rather not take advantage of these opportunities please tick box ☐